Lavender and Steel

E. WAYNE CUNDIFF

To Edie & Brother Bob!
Thanks for availing
your sister to our cribbage club.
Best Wishes,
E. Wayne Cundiff
"Ed"

PAGE PUBLISHING, INC.
New York, NY

First originally published by Page Publishing, Inc. 2018

This book is a work of fiction. Any resemblance to any persons, living or dead, is coincidental.
This work contains a number of pejorative terms for various groups of people. Please understand that the words are used in context, and do not reflect the sentiments of the author.

ISBN 978-1-64298-498-9 (Paperback)
ISBN 978-1-64298-499-6 (Digital)

Printed in the United States of America

To everyone who ever befriended me,
especially in my loneliest times.

1

Mid-1980s

EAMON CUDAHY PUSHED himself out of bed on a restful Sunday morning in Northern Arizona. Since many were not sure how to pronounce that first name, and in an effort to assimilate, he just had everyone call him Ed. He felt around the spare tire of his midriff, partly resentful and partly thankful he was not as overweight as he had been as a child and teen. Rubbing his fingers through his still-red hair, starting to gray, and roughing up his beard, he tracked into the kitchen to see what his wife, Eileen, had going. Ed and Eileen had met in college, waited three years to get married, and were now on their third year of marriage, both with stable jobs, but no kids yet.

His wife spoke in her upbeat tone, "Hey, sweetheart. There's an article about a murder in Phoenix. Suspect was a professor from our alma mater." Ed picked up the paper, wondering, *Maybe? Could it be that imbalanced teacher of mine from about ten years ago?* Ed shook his head. He knew never to jump to conclusions, a lesson he had learned from the many history books he had read and studied, and six years of teaching the subject. He picked up the newspaper and glanced at the article. Eileen heard that moan, almost a sigh, and recognized it as one of her husband's muted gasps when faced with something painful or disturbing.

"What is it?" Eileen asked. "Did you know him?"

Ed nodded his head. "Yes . . . that teacher I mentioned a few times that I had troubles with. I always thought he was weird, to say the least, and homosexual, but nothing like this."

What Cudahy read the next few minutes sounded stranger than anything he had read in his assortment of cop novels, and even rivaled the books he had read about serial killers and phantoms of the past like Jack the Ripper. Remains had been found, and an investigation led back to the apartment and house of one Francis DeSales Mackey, long-time history professor at Phoenix State University. Mackey offered no comment, but police said they had arrested the suspect the night before, advised him of his rights, and that he was now undergoing questioning.

The article also described the victim, a seventeen-year-old runaway from Owensboro, Kentucky, Travis Neughton Kingman, a known street urchin, previously arrested for juvenile offenses and drugs. A physical description followed: white male, muscular build, with tattoos and a Mohawk-style haircut. So far, only the torso and head had been located.

Another coincidence, though not as startling—Ed's father's family was from Kentucky, and Ed had lived in Louisville through fourth and fifth grade before being uprooted again and hauled across country to the desert of Arizona. Ed often regretted that his family had moved from there, some of the happiest days of his childhood. Then again, things had turned out well once Ed found a good job and the right woman.

Ed finished reading the article, then shaved and showered in preparation for mass. His mind often wandered in church, but this morning was a real challenge, trying to follow the homily while images of his former professor danced around in his mind, and trying to imagine the gruesome circumstances that led up to the murder and dismemberment of a young man.

Later in the afternoon, Ed called up his old friend Dan from his dorm days. They had remained good pals over the years, and kept in touch.

"Hey, there, Dan, it's old Ed from State."

"Good to hear from you," Dan chimed in.

The two chums chatted briefly, and finally Ed asked, "Say, there must be a lot in your local paper about a prof from our school who is up on charges of murder one?"

"You bet . . . everyone's talking about it. It's on the TV, and . . . did you know him or what?" Dan asked.

"Real well. He taught history, and we had many run-ins, largely unpleasant ones, and I took him for a space case, but never dreamed of this."

"No kidding—can't imagine actually knowing someone that demented," his friend concurred.

"Grisly, that's the word," Ed added.

"That's the word, all right, along with lots of others. Did you want me to send you the clippings?" Dan knew his old friend well.

"Exactly what I was thinking. Do that, and we can talk more when you and I hook up sometime soon."

Ed hung up the phone and sat in his old, beat-up recliner, a hand-me-down from his dad. He chewed on what he had just read, pictured the man who had caused him such grief ten years earlier, when Ed was just twenty-one, trying to make it through college. As much as he loved history, the hoops he had to jump through with some classes ate at him, and Mackey's class was the worst of all, almost ending his quest for a degree.

But Ed had survived, and after a series of unhappy jobs, returned to college to seek a teaching credential, with still more hoops, but he had made it! He had landed a great job, teaching history at an all-girls' Catholic high school a few hours north of where he had attended college and lived since he was eleven. Not much money, but great students, lots of vacation time, and a short commute.

He closed his eyes. The image of his old professor was clear. He could still see the face and hear the voice of Professor Mackey, or "Wacky Mackey," as others called him behind his back, and feel the intensity of the man, his condescending attitude and effeminate demeanor.

What drove Mackey to this butchery? How did a teenager end up in Mackey's tangled web? There could not be an easy answer, but

Ed remained haunted by the specter of his old nemesis, and felt some sympathy for the victim, whoever he was. Always one to reminisce, Ed thought back to those uncertain years of college.

2

Ten years before the murder.

E D FUMBLED WITH his new class schedule and trekked out to the Social Studies buildings he had known too well as a history major. He breathed the cool air, a rarity in Phoenix, on a January evening. When he started college, Ed thought he would prefer night classes, since he liked to sleep in late as a high schooler, but now, arriving at dark seemed depressing, especially in this gloom. He could hear two cats moaning at each other, and wondered what their dialogue was about. He entered the hallway just before seven and looked for the classroom. Through a glass window in the door, crisscrossed with that wire to prevent breakage, he raised up slightly (at five nine, an inch or two made a difference) to glance in. He looked behind him and saw a pretty black girl with skin the color of coffee with a lot of cream that he knew casually from other classes—not a big coincidence since they had the same major. Ed fished through his memory bank for her name. Girls were a minority in the history department, and she was a minority in the racial sense, so it came to him.

"Oh, hi, Lawanda, looks like we have a class together again." Lawanda smiled amiably and nodded. She joined Ed in peering through the window to get a gander at their new prof, one they had only barely heard about. The middle-aged man, average height and build, was sloppily dressed in baggy pants, shirt, and sweater whose colors did not match, and a wool hat with tufts of hair sticking out, and he also needed a shave. To say he looked slovenly would be an

9

understatement. Ed thought about the word *professorial* he had heard in his childhood, conjuring an image of a distinguished gentleman in a tweed coat smoking a pipe, and could not think of anything more contradictory than what he was viewing.

Lawanda grimaced and spoke to Ed in a disgusted tone, "Ohhh, does he always wear that wig?" Remembering that girls usually noticed such things, Ed focused on the sporadic hairs and thought that, *Yeah, I guess that is a wig.* Being a teenager in the early '70s, when even wealthy kids were into the grubby look and disdained slacks and long-sleeved shirts and instead donned faded jeans and army attire, Ed decided not to put too much store in his new teacher's appearance. He, like most other youth of the late hippy era, would often say that dressing up made no difference in anyone's competence or character. Ed, a slimmed-down version of his former self, ambled into the classroom and took a desk in the front corner near the door and prepared to take in whatever words the disheveled history professor had to expound.

As class began, the shabbily dressed and bespectacled man introduced himself. "I am Dr. Mackey, a professor and member of the department since 1968." Mackey spoke with a lisp and moved about restlessly, displaying effeminate body language, and his words were muttered softly. All those mannerisms reminded Ed of Truman Capote, whom he had seen on TV talk shows and did impersonations of to make his friends laugh. That was Ed, all right, with loads of sadness in his life, but always trying to be the clown. Sitting in that class now, at age twenty-one, worrying about his future, he still hoped to make everyone else laugh by being a jokester. Some resented him for that, but for Ed, a basically shy type who had been ridiculed through his childhood for his obesity, red hair and social ineptness, the humor was both a shield and a leaning post. So Ed quietly listened, best he could, to the droning, irritating tone that Mackey took, not just effeminate, but nasal and obnoxious.

By the end of the class, there had been no imparting of knowledge or historical technique, just a poorly worded syllabus and a lot of rambling comments by Mackey, who wandered off topic and talked about his experiences, even one in which he claimed to have gotten on the bad side of a Navajo chieftain, who cursed Mackey with the impending baldness now creeping up on him. Ed was later to learn that Mackey had also had a hair transplant which had not taken well and made the professor look more haphazard than ever.

Ed began to make his silent departure from the classroom when Mackey caught his attention in a voice soft but annoying.

"And have I seen you at other history department functions?"

"Oh, maybe so, Dr. Mackey, this is my third year." Ed always tried to speak respectfully, especially to someone older and in a position of authority.

"You live in the dorms. I saw you approaching from the commons. Are you from elsewhere, originally?" Mackey asked.

"I'm from Mesa," he responded. Not entirely true. Ed had moved all over the country as a navy brat, living even in Cuba and Canada, before his old dad bailed out at age thirty-nine, avoiding a cruise to Vietnam just before the war took off in full force. After a failed attempt to live in Kentucky because Ed's mother was unhappy with her husband's constant boozing, which she blamed on her in-laws, they ended up in Mesa. And no surprise, the old man kept up his alcoholism, so the move out West accomplished nothing, except that both Ed and his older sister lost good friends and ended up in a much less happy setting.

"Oh, I like Mesa, those palm trees downtown," Mackey intoned with that weasel voice of his, biting on the words, making them more unpleasant, and nodded to Ed in some degree of attempted friendship.

"Yes, that is scenic." He did not know how else to converse with his teacher, but smiled at the prof and headed back to the dorms.

As he meandered through the quiet of the night, Ed wondered about this strange and intriguing man. Maybe Mackey could not help his speech—it might be some sort of impediment, and he reminded himself of the folly of judging by appearance. Still, the young guy had a feeling in his gut that Dr. Mackey would play a major part in his life, somehow, someday.

3

AFTER A MONTH or so, Ed was growing dreary of his nighttime class with the abrasive professor. This was not a new experience for him, since he often just got fed up with pointless classes, but Mackey's droning and venting had gotten the best of him. Teachers often digressed, but Mackey used class time to bellyache about his political views (all far left-wing) and never addressed the topic of the class which, admittedly, was nebulous by name—"Overview of the Historical Process." But Ed heard his classmates grumbling, not just about Mackey's weirdo personality (that was the word most often applied—"weirdo"), but his failure to deliver anything worth jotting down in a notebook or indicating to his students what might be on the midterm.

"I haven't learned *shit* in Mackey's class," his friend Eric stated bluntly.

And then there were other comments. "Mackey? I heard that dude's gay!"

Gay was still a fairly new term in the seventies, and Ed never used it but was starting to think his worst enemy in the department was not straight. "He doesn't like girls" was often noted, but that was not quite right. Mackey was responsive to the hardcore women's libbers in the class, who seized every opportunity to condemn males, blaming them for the ills of society and claiming that everything positive in history had actually been the work of women. He would always address the feminists by saying, "And you are Mizz . . ." stretching out the *z* sound of that title, Ms., just coming into vogue.

Some professors were slaves to their lesson plans, to the point where their lectures sounded canned and overly rehearsed, but what the unconventional teacher tossed out had no direction or goals. Thus Ed, a daydreamer by nature, could not pay the least bit of attention in class. If he had listened, it probably would not have done him any good anyhow. For example, he did not know a break had been called one evening until he saw his fellow students heading out to the hallway and outdoors for a talk or a smoke.

Ten minutes later, Ed returned to his desk in the corner, and a tune was stilled lodged in his head. He had no musical talent, but always had songs going on in his mind, and tried to sing when no one could listen, which they would not want to do. So it was Ed's misfortune to be sitting in Mackey's class, shortly before he resumed his preaching, that Ed was softly whistling, barely audible, but close enough to Mackey for him to hear and respond.

For the first time since junior high school, when Ed had been a moderate discipline problem, he found himself being ordered out into the hallway for a chewing out. Being yelled at was nothing new to him, with a navy chief for a father who would tear into him like a new recruit at the slightest provocation, but this was scary; the one on his case now had a power over Ed—the grade.

"I don't know if you're trying to be a smart *ass*, or what," Mackey began in that nasal and irritating tone of his, the words searing into Ed, causing him to squirm. The professor continued his harangue, lisping and sputtering. The words "smart ass" sounded like they were bitten through a barbed wire.

"I haven't quite finished grading the essays from the last exam," Mackey continued, "but it looks like you might just have failed. Most people in this subject just eat it up, but it could just be you are in the wrong major."

Those last words stung Ed. More than halfway through college, he deemed it impossible to change majors and start all over again. He was one of the few who vowed to graduate at twenty-two, not thirty-two like some he had known. Besides, he felt belittled, under attack by someone who failed to deliver anything of significance in his classroom.

They returned to class, and Ed simmered a while. He feared the end of the semester and how a low grade would wreck his GPA and set his goal of graduation back. Worse, he hated taking fire from someone he had now no respect for.

Cudahy retraced his steps through the bleak night, returning to the commons dorm hall he liked so much. There was always someone to talk to, hopefully one to confide in and offer reassurance. Though it was late, he encountered a friend, Mick Garner, a journalism major with a good listening ear. Ed laid down the account of the thrashing from his history prof, someone Mick had never met, but he listened in sympathy.

"He could be right about you being in the wrong major," Mick offered.

"I hope not. Invested too much time and money to turn back—just have to forge ahead," Ed explained.

Mick spoke up, "Oh, I just remembered something . . . from someone else Mackey tore into. Can't remember his name, but another journalism guy who had him for a lower-level history class. Guy was sitting at his desk, munching the crushed ice from the Coke he had brought in after break, and the sound of the chewing really pissed off Mackey. He hauled him out, like he did to you, made all kinds of accusations, that this guy made the noise deliberately to be a smart ass, and then"—imitating Mackey's speech and stance, dangling his fingers in front of him—"'You have been making dithparaging remarkth about the way I dreth'—that sort of crap. So you're not the only one."

The two dormies nodded to each other, and Ed fell into bed, careful not to awaken his roommate, Dana. In spite of his gloom, Ed felt some comfort in knowing what a good roommate he had in Dana, a crim major with a big heart and keen sense of humor. He drifted into restless sleep and hoped to wake up the next morning in brighter spirits.

4

One year later.

S O I DID it, Ed thought, graduated in four years, age twenty-two, and not floundering like so many of his friends, some of whom were older but still had not garnered even one semester of units. He had feared Mackey's wrath, but assuaged it by appealing to the man's pride. He knew that if he asked Mackey for advice, the professor would view him more favorably and grade more mercifully. He was right, too. He had approached Mackey after class, humbly asked for some directions and suggestions for research and pointers on how to interview primary sources, and the little jerk had eaten it up. Ed got his report card, let out a sigh of relief when he saw the *C*, and knew he could skate by to graduation.

But not without the annual visit to Mackey's private residence, not far from campus. Every year, Mackey would invite the students from his upper division class to his home for a final wrap-up session, with no particular purpose. Ed biked over to the large house in a respectable neighborhood and could not believe the front yard, covered with concrete. *Probably just does not want to mow the lawn, or even have somebody else do it. I bet his neighbors never speak to him,* he thought to himself.

The score or so of history students sat in the spacious living room, cross-legged on the floor, guru-style, and let Mackey preach to them, appealing to his massive ego. The one event that stood out most in everyone's mind was when one of the students started down

15

a hallway in search of the bathroom and headed toward one door, when Mackey jumped up, almost in hysterics, and yelled at him, "***Don't* go in there!**"

The words sounded frantic, and the look on Mackey's face showed primal fear. What was behind that door? Rumors persisted for years that the forbidden room must have been the professor's "House of Horrors," replete with torture chambers, chains, whips, and mirrors.

In the months following graduation, Ed would sometimes drop by the history department, sometimes in search of a job prospect or just to shoot the breeze with his favorite teacher, Dr. Freeman, a personable and easygoing sort, the opposite of Mackey. Dr. Freeman would sometimes ask Ed a trivia question about the presidents or history, especially if there were other history profs in his office, and Ed never let him down. "I *knew* he'd know that!" Freeman would guffaw.

And then there were those encounters with Mackey, which he tried to avoid, but had nonetheless. Once, while submitting some items, he ventured into Mackey's shared office to borrow a stapler and heard, "Oh, Ed, you always are a person in need," making Ed feel uncomfortable. Many times, Mackey would say, "And you are the only person I know who whistles in class."

Those comments were irritating, but nothing compared to Mackey's golden opportunity, as he must have seen it, to pounce on Ed. At one point, Ed had dropped by to see Dr. Freeman, got snagged by Mackey, who asked if Ed knew of anyone seeking a job with a historical research company (knowing full well Ed was job hunting.)

"Well . . . oh . . . I would love to look into a position like that," Ed spoke with some hesitation.

Mackey almost exploded in disbelief and spoke loudly, with exaggerated disdain, "Oh no, I wouldn't *dare* recommend *you* for this job, not *you*, it requires . . . " He went on with qualities that he felt Ed apparently lacked, making Ed feel small.

It would have been hard for most people to keep a civil tongue at this moment, but Ed had trouble with confrontations, and just kept quiet, thinking to himself, *He knew I was looking for work, he brought up that position knowing that fully well, and he responded with such exaggerated surprise and disgust,* and realized . . . *the little queer set me up for that insult.*

As he walked down the hallway, steaming, it came to him what he should have said, if he had had the nerve, and thought of it in time—"And you know what, Dr. Mackey? I wouldn't recommend you for a teacher, either."

Those words remained unsaid, but never forgotten. Someone as abrasive and undercutting as Professor Mackey would leave a quiet guy like Ed with a lot of bitter memories and unresolved conflict churning inside him. Always one to dwell in the past, a bad habit of his, the insults and condescension of the slovenly teacher would shadow him.

5

Travis—the spring before the murder.

TRAVIS KINGMAN STARED out the window of the bus as it rolled along a country highway, watching the rows of crops that looked like a wagon wheel spinning in front of him, if he kept his eyes still. He had never been this far from Owensboro, but the land did not look too much different, passing through Missouri, he thought, but not sure. He had paid for the ticket with money he made by selling his grandfather's gold coin collection, which he had stolen on his way out. His family would never forgive him, he figured, but who cared? All he wanted was out.

He reached up, rubbed his hands over his mostly shaved head, and preened the Mohawk into a more vertical position. Looking like a punker would help him, he thought, appear tougher and scarier. That, and the tattoos the old white supremacist gang had given him last year. He was intimidating enough already, at six feet three, buff build, and a mean look that made just about anyone think twice about challenging him.

The bus glided along, smooth without many hills, and signs that said things like "Joplin, two hundred miles." He could barely read, not write or spell worth a hoot, and Travis wondered about his future. He would make it in the movies—his strong face and long, muscular body would shoe him in so slick—and all the crap he left behind in Owensboro would mean nothing. His dad had died, his mom too sad to deal with it, and brothers long gone. So California

18

was the place for him, a place where it was always warm, and everyone lived by the ocean, something he had never seen. He closed his eyes, tried to picture his new home and new friends, and drifted off to sleep.

After about two-and-a-half days on the road, Travis finally bailed out when he got to Hollywood. What he saw was not movie stars strolling down the street, but every kind of wacko he ever imagined—people dressed as comic book heroes, guys dressed up like women, and hardcore drug users. Travis had seen plenty of dopers in his time, had fiddled with drugs himself, but the crack use alone seemed more than he could grasp.

At a nearby diner, Travis ordered a pile of pancakes and ate them up quickly, chugging buttermilk to wash it down. He liked that, close to Kentucky food, and checked out the waitress serving him—she had to be older than Travis, just turned seventeen himself, but he tried to engage her in talk. Politely, she let him know she was off limits, but he decided to ask her the most important question on his mind.

"Where do you go to try out for a part in a movie?"

She smiled, with a look of "I've heard that so many times," and told him, "You and a few million others—there are studios not far from here, but getting anyone to consider you, even, is pretty tough." She gave him the same general directions she gave to all the other Hollywood hopefuls she had encountered in the past. Travis left a small tip and headed out to the busy sidewalk.

He followed her directions to a movie studio and waited in a long line of nervous fumblers, mostly young, holding folders with—? Travis wondered if he needed pictures of himself, or whatever the other wannabes held in their arms.

After a long and tedious wait, Travis finally made it to the head of the line and faced a grumpy-looking stiff who barely looked up at him. The old-timer was short and squat, wearing polyester pants, and smelled of that ointment his dad had always smelled of, something for his rear.

"You in the union?" he asked in an unfriendly voice.

Travis did not know what a union was, thought of the word *Union*, to mean the North during the Civil War, figured that was on the wrong track, and just shook his head.

"Come back when you got a card," the stiff grumbled at him.

A card for what? His mind tumbled a bit, and he felt, already, that his quest for stardom was being denied before it was even attempted. Still baffled, he walked slowly through the crowds of tourists, voyeurs, and regulars. After a while, he fell into a casual conversation with a group of punkers who told him about a place where they made dirty movies, would hire anybody who looked halfway good. "Just file in. Maybe you'll get something," one of them encouraged him.

So Travis sauntered down the seedy streets of Hollywood until he found the studio the punkers had described to him—run down, looked more like an old hardware store, but through the dusty windows he could make out some desks and other young people sitting along the walls in plastic chairs. He filled out a brief form, which took him a while, with his scrawling, and then joined the others.

A middle-aged man in loud clothes and snow-white hair styled in a pompadour came from out of the back and took a look around the room. Spotting Travis, he let out a gasp, turned on his heel and went back to quarters, and returned quickly with someone who could have passed for his brother.

"Phil, look at him! That's what we need for Dominita, her next video! You think?"

"Maybe, Terry, maybe . . . let's invite him back for a chat."

Within minutes, Travis was seated behind an old desk, sitting in a ratty chair, listening to two sleazy shysters who fed him lots of compliments and offered him a role in a short flick.

"You don't have to say or do much . . . just play the victim. The star is a dominatrix," the one named Phil told him.

Kingman's blank face told them he had no idea what that word meant.

"You know, a woman who likes to slap men around, boss them, make them feel like shit, 'cause some guys dig it. A fantasy. Big guy like you, with your Mohawk, will make a perfect victim. Interested?" Phil's brother, maybe, Terry asked.

"Sure," Travis answered softly. This could be his break, he needed the money, and what to lose?

Phil pointed off to his left and said, "Okay, so go down the hall to the left, and our makeup girl will get you ready."

Travis did as he was told and ended up in a shabby room with a girl that had a bored look on her face and a clipboard in her hands.

Without introducing herself, she told him, "Okay, I'll get some makeup on you, then you get into your outfit. It's over there—just put on the collar and the boxers."

Travis sat stolidly while she applied some powder to his face and touched up his eyes. The collar was just a large dog collar, and the shorts were, with huge polka dots, like those worn in old TV sitcoms. There were metal studs around the collar and a leash attached. What the hell, he got into his outfit.

He proceeded to the set, walked in, and saw large lights, cameras, and his costar, who almost defied description. She was dressed in shiny silver chains, the lower ones wrapped around her like a jock, showing her butt cheeks, and the upper ones trailing up her front and looped around her neck. Her coal-black hair was heavily hair sprayed, with the sort of mascara and eye shadow that the hoody girls in high school had worn, only more so. She wore black leather gloves (really plastic) that went up to her elbows, and matching boots up to her thighs, with high heels. The heels, added to her already substantial height, made her about as tall as Travis. In her hand she held what looked like a riding crop with thick black ribbons.

Sitting nearby on a sofa were two short girls, who looked like munchkins near their mistress. The first munchkin wore steel-toe construction boots. Her almost twin wore gloves with fake spikes painted silver that were actually rubber. They weren't wearing anything else.

The two sleazes appeared at this point to coach Travis.

"Okay, Trevor, we have some pointers."

"Travis."

"Oh, yeah. Travis. First, get that tough-guy look off your face. You have to look scared. When she orders you, look terrified and nod your head like you are begging for mercy."

Sleaze Number Two joined in. "When she hits you, make it look painful, and fall down, or over, so you will look helpless. And take these."

Travis held what looked like two capsules of drugs he had abused over the years.

Sleaze Number One explained to him, "Those are fake blood capsules. Put one along your gum line and bite it when you get hit. Put the other up one nostril and push on it sometime later. Got it?

Travis nodded to show he got it and watched while the lights were positioned and two camera men readied for the action. He stood in the center of the set, tried to look helpless—which he was, really—and the tall woman and her two minions writhed around him. When someone called, "Action!" she jumped to life and snarled into the camera.

"I am Dominita, the Duchess of Domination, and all you pitiful piles of dog shit will obey my every word! Who is this sniveling loser brought to me now?"

As if on cue, Travis began to speak. "My name—"

Dominita back fisted him on the cheek, causing the capsule to spurt out, prematurely, and dribble down his chin.

"Shut your face, maggot! *I* tell you when to talk, when to do anything, you stupid mamma's boy—that goes for all you losers, my sorry sacks of manure, too wimpy to stand up for yourselves!" Her words were a mixture of plosives and hissing, with a heavy emphasis on the *s* in any word.

She started whipping him with the black plastic ribbons, and Travis stumbled, pretending to be hurt, while she continued with a barrage of insults, spiced with slaps to his face and kicks to his legs. The two munchkins sprinkled him with punches and stomps.

Dominita screamed, "Crawl on your belly, slave! Do what I say, and tell me you like it!"

Not knowing what to do, Travis nodded his head and tried to act like he was begging for more. She yanked the leash, forcing his head back, and Travis felt strangled and dizzy.

"Bow to me, you gutless turd, NOW!"

Travis tried to bow, as he may have done in a square dance, and she kneed him in the forehead, causing a dull pain, causing him to lose his balance.

After a few more minutes of verbal and physical abuse, she yelled out to her two assistants. "Boots! Spike! Finish him off!"

Boots lived up to her name, kicking him in the side, not with any power, but the steel-toed boots registered. "Spike," as she was called, delivered rabbit punches to the back of his head. Travis pushed in on one nostril, and the fake blood trickled down over his mouth.

One of the snow-haired sleazes motioned to cut the filming and entered the foray.

"Turn over on your back," he instructed. Travis obeyed, something he had gotten used to, and the other sleaze poured shiny red liquid on his chest that looked more like fingernail polish than blood. He called the three women over and instructed them on the closing scene.

When the cameras were rolling again, Travis was on his back, with the dominatrix standing over him, one high heel on his chest, making him look like an animal that had just been shot and claimed. The two girls circled around him, pointing at him and laughing in the tone used for ridiculing someone.

She looked down at the helpless Travis and snarled, "You will always obey me! I will command your every move! Don't ever think you have any reason to exist except for my hand on the whip, you weak, impotent . . . ASSHOLE!" The last word was shouted with a heavy tone of condescension.

After Travis got up, and started to clean himself, he heard her voice barking into a camera—

"There is a phone number on the bottom of the screen. Write it down, slaves, and call me, that's an order, and speak to Dominita any time, day or night. Till then, kneel to me and kiss my feet!"

The two directors, if that's what they were, gathered around casually.

"Good job, Doris. You and the girls take a break, get ready for another later in the day. We're looking for a mousy accountant type next shoot."

The other white-haired partner patted Travis on the shoulder in a friendly manner. "You did good, Trevor. On your way out, ask the girl at the counter for your pay envelope, and come back in a month or so. We'll see if we have anything for you."

Being called by the wrong name mattered little. Travis just wanted to leave and grab whatever money he had coming to him. A tired blond handed him an envelope and he peeked into it—five twenty-dollar bills. The most money he had ever made in an hour. Sure beat washing dishes at his old job at the Keona. But only once a month, at best? He pondered what other means he had to survive.

Some of the locals told him about a fleabag hotel called Parkinson's, where the rooms were cheap, and if you slipped the clerk a five, he skipped the check for ID. He found the hotel, checked in, noted the hookers and pimps gathered in the trashy diner, and rested in his room that smelled of old odors and some cleanser that tried to eliminate it. He dozed off after some restless stirring and thought to himself, *What a shithole.*

The next day, Travis wandered, looking for someplace to pick up some money. He spotted a bar with a long name he could not read, but the pale purple paint on the exterior made him think he had found what he wanted. It was the same shade his Aunt Ollie liked so much, the color of her favorite apron, that she told him was lavender. As he walked around the bar, and into an alley, he saw two words spray painted on the side, graffiti-style, that he could read—"FAG BAR." Yep, this would work.

For the next week or so, he would loiter around, looking lost, and the patrons would spot him, sometimes striking up a conversation, then propositioning him. A twenty here, once in a while a fifty, just so they could play with him. There were pretty boys from the college, just a few years his senior, who offered him joints, pills, or snorts, all of which he accepted. He continued this soliciting, hoping for the situation to improve, but it dragged on.

One afternoon, while pacing in front of the bar with the too-challenging name, he heard, faintly, a voice behind him.

"Son?"

He turned to see a man, very short, dressed all in shades of bland gray, trying to get his attention. Travis was baffled—no small talk, no "Well, looks like you could use a friend," as the little man reached back and pulled out a wallet. This confused Travis even more, to think he was being offered money before any discussion.

What Travis saw next shocked him, as the wallet flipped open for his viewing—a bright and shiny gold badge. He had been badged before, busted for shoplifting dating back to eighth grade and later possession and selling, landing him in juvie for a while, but what was this? This guy did not look like any law enforcement Travis had ever seen, and took him by surprise.

The cop, or security guard, or whatever he was, walked alongside him slowly, and asked one question—"What's your name?"

"Uh, sir, I didn't steal anything."

"*What's* your name?"

"I don't have any drugs on me." That was the truth—Travis used them up as soon as he got them.

The short man's voice took a breathier, yet somehow more threatening tone—"All right, I've asked you twice, I'll ask you one . . . more . . . time . . ." adding some assertiveness to the tone— "*what's . . . your . . . name?*"

Hanging his head in submission, he answered. "Travis Kingman," and dreaded the thought of being sent back home.

Little man nodded, and Travis pleaded—"What is this? I haven't done anything," as they walked, it seemed with an aim, across one street and down the other.

Without looking at Travis, he answered, "I work vice around here. I know what you're doing. But it's not poor street kids I'm after. It's the older guys that I can put in prison. So I'm giving you a break."

Those words lifted Travis's spirits—he was not going to get locked up then sent back to Owensboro.

The man in gray continued, "See that building there? That's the Hollywood bus depot. Hop on any bus and head out of town, any direction, and I never see you again. If I do, then it's handcuffs and the whole nine yards. Got it?"

Travis got it, for sure, and entered the ugly depot and stood in line at a ticket booth. Good thing he had been carrying his backpack at the time, with the bulk of his few belongings with him, not back at the hotel.

"Destination?" the woman behind the counter asked.

"What's the next bus out?"

She had heard that question before, looked up at a display, and said, "Phoenix," and points east.

"Okay, Phoenix."

Taking the ticket, he sat briefly, then boarded the bus, just like the one that had brought him to Hollywood, and found an empty seat. He heard the familiar drone of the motor, and a sweet smell that all such buses seemed to have. Shortly after, he heard a voice like the host of a children's show.

"Pardon me, young fellow, is this seat spoken for?"

Travis shook his head, and the slightly chubby forty-something man settled in. After a few minutes of slight discomfort, the man asked him about where he was headed, and other general questions, but specifically, "By any chance, were you rousted from Hollywood?"

"'Rousted'?"

"You know, as they would have said in the Old West, 'run out of town by the sheriff'?" The passenger spoke these words with a lilt and a faint smile.

"Yeah, something like that," Travis responded hesitantly.

"I thought so—the Hollywood police can be intolerant. I saw you being escorted over here, as I looked out the window, by an officious looking gent. My name is Walt Bello."

"Travis Kingman." And they shook hands. Travis tried to imagine Phoenix and whether his fellow passenger would be just an acquaintance or had some greater meaning for his future.

6

Ed, twenty years before the murder.

WELL, HERE I go again, Ed Cudahy thought to himself as he ambled down the dusty road with no sidewalk and weeds that fed up to the railroad tracks. For the seventh time in his eleven years, he was the "new kid" again, and would have to struggle for acceptance. Not easy; besides the usual resistance to a newcomer, he was overweight, wore his hair too short, and suffered from some social ineptitude, not uncommon for the child of an alcoholic. At least this wasn't as bad as last Spring, when his family suddenly departed Kentucky and ended up at one school, more than three-fifths through the school year. To win acceptance at that school, Ed had become a comedian in the most absurd sense of the word, hoping his classmates would accept him.

Then, they moved again, this time to a different part of town, where he spent the entire summer alone. The old saying, "You don't have a friend in the world," was more than just a saying. He sat in the house almost all day, waking up at noon and watching old reruns, never speaking to anyone other than the immediate members of his family (and not much) and brief words to store cashiers when they went out shopping, or he had to get a haircut— every two weeks in those days.

So he continued his walk to the new school, hoping to make friends and be accepted, always a challenge. As he approached the campus, he saw something quite different from his last two schools.

Not an old red brick building, or dull gray halls, but a more west-ern-style school with bungalows and no enclosed areas, the way they would have been in Kentucky or any place east of the Mississippi. Willard Elementary, room 12, the card in his hand read, and he waited alone for eight fifteen to come. Many students were socializ-ing, catching up on what had happened over the summer, and Ed felt even more alone. He eventually took a place at the back of the boys' line (that would never happen again after sixth grade) and stared at the blacktop.

The boy in front of him turned slightly and said, "Are you new?"

Ed nodded, no words, and returned his focus to the blacktop. They shuffled in and were greeted, solemnly, by a severe-looking and very overweight woman dressed completely in black.

Every student took a seat, with each desk marked by a piece of cardboard taped on the top with the student's name on it. After some restless shifting, the stout woman addressed the class in what Ed rec-ognized as a New York accent, similar to his mother's. The tone was haughty, with that hint of a superior attitude so many of his teachers had had.

"I am Mrs. Broker. Please take your seats and be quiet." She seemed standoffish, almost arrogant, and Ed knew her type already. He doubted if his new teacher would like him. Some in the past had, others had not, but his gut told him this was one of those teach-ers who felt it obligatory to put students down, especially boys, and would never acknowledge his good points. All of his intuitions turned out to be right.

As the first days passed, he felt the usual stiffness of being new and unknown, excluded, but especially became the focus of one of the most assertive boys, Tom Kellogg, not exactly the class clown, but the one seemingly in charge of taunting and making Ed feel like a loser. Tom persisted with insults about Ed's weight and general awk-wardness. Ed knew what this meant, one of two things: he could just keep on turning away, submissively, or engage in a fight with his new enemy.

Both choices were unacceptable. His dad always told him, "When you're new, figure out who's the toughest kid in class, pick a fight with him, kick his ass, or fight to a standstill. All problems will be over. The guys will say you're all right, one of *us*, and pat you on the back . . . "

But Ed never learned to fight, did not have the heart or stomach for it, and was the type to avoid confrontations of any kind, but the critical moment came one day after school at in the middle of the second week.

Ed was about to leave for home when his nemesis, Tom, began teasing him and pulling at this shirt just beyond the classroom area. Now or never, Ed thought, so he finally pounced on Tom and applied a bear hug around his fairly skinny opponent. Ed was definitely stronger than Tom and made an effort to crush him with his arms, but the two almost danced around the shrubbery as Tom struggled to get loose, which he eventually did, and swung at Ed with what was more of a slap than a punch.

Like usual, Ed lost his nerve and broke, started to cry, much to his own dismay and embarrassment. Tom showed some sympathy, glad the encounter was over, and made peace, offered possibly some degree of friendship, with the new guy. It was not just between Ed and Tom. In most classes, there is one boy who is socially dominant over the others—the "alpha male." Ed did not know that term at eleven but knew that Dale, the most athletic and self-confident of all the boys, pretty much ruled all schoolyard activities. Thus, Dale the alpha male, chimed in and also offered some friendship to Ed, and some implied acceptance.

The three of them walked down Spring Street toward home and exchanged friendly talk, some laughs and smiles. The gap had closed between the new kid and the two most prominent boys, and the year would turn out better. As they parted toward different destinations, Tom and Dale both called out,

"See you, Ed!" in a tone that made Ed realize that the ice had been broken, and the worst of his struggle was over.

The weeks rolled by, and Ed was still looking for a best friend, someone to hang out with at lunch and recess. After some uncertainty, he began friendly banter with Bryce, a mild-mannered sort with glasses, who spoke in a soft voice and had a great sense of humor, which he shared with Ed. Bryce was an avid fan of entertainment, and he and Ed would meet in the morning before school and discuss their favorite TV shows and latest movies. Ed tended to give nick-names to his friends and enemies both, and for Bryce, it was "Bryce-a-roni," or "Bryce Canyon." Bryce would always smile when called that, and it helped strengthen the bond forming between the two.

Bryce invited Ed over to his house one afternoon. Ed always thought of that invitation as a more concrete definition of a friend, not just a school chum. Bryce had a flair for jokes, and told them in a highly theatrical voice, with gestures and inflections, foreshadowing the actor that Bryce would later become.

"Hey, Ed, have you heard this one?" Striking up an animated persona, and effecting a Mexican accent, Bryce broke into a song. "My name ees El Pancho, I work at El Rancho, I earn ten pesos a day . . . I go to *Meeeees Loooosy*, and play weeth her *poooosy*, she takes my ten pesos away—*OLÉ*." The *olé* included a spirited hand waving for accentuation, and a tone of resignation.

Ed laughed, more at Bryce's antics than the joke; not being a native of the West, this ridicule of Mexicans was new to him. In Kentucky, there were similar jokes, but about blacks.

This new form of racism puzzled him. One day after class, he was approaching the corner in front of the school, about to cross the street, when one of his classmates, Scott, put an arm out like a turn-pike and insisted he stop. In front of the arm stood a younger boy, darker, and Scott's warning to Ed was audible to all three of them.

"He's a beaner—don't get too close to him."

Ed had never heard the word *beaner*, only guessed at its mean-ing, and was surprised. Scott had always been a nice sort, nicknamed "Scott Tissue," and just smiled when called that. Ed filed the incident away in his mind, learning that racism took a different angle out here in Arizona.

Becoming accepted by his classmates was a goal never fully achieved. Being the best reader and speller in class did not count, he already knew, but what exactly put a kid at the top, or near the top, of the social ladder? There were the "cool guys"—the most asser-tive, the most self-confident—and then there were the losers, which included Ed, the fat klutz with poor social skills, and Bryce, passive and soft by nature. Of course, being good at sports always helped, which explained why Dale and Tom largely ruled Mrs. Broker's class, and why Ed, the bungler, took a back row.

As usual, Ed tried to gain popularity by humor, being the funny guy. The jokes the sixth graders told so frequently all reeked of immaturity and ended with lines like, "Dr. Bennet! Dr. Bennett!"

"Ben' it, hell, I broke it!"

"Rectum? He damn near killed 'im!" and, "Ahh, bald-headed rat!"

It worked, to a small degree, especially his one joke that seemed hilarious in sixth grade but idiotic at any later stage in life. He told it at least three dozen times to various assembled groups before school, a puerile and overtly racist tale about a little black kid, a horny white lady, her jealous husband, and the oft-repeated quote, also the punchline, "Fo' a nickel Ah weel!" It brought gales of raucous laughter and a portion of the acceptance Ed craved.

And what about the girls? It seemed they also split into two camps right before school started each morning, when groups milled around, talking, and dictating where you sat in the cafeteria or outside lunch benches. The cuter girls made up the prominent group, while the others—chubby, homely, plain or awkward—gathered among themselves. It was that second group that Mrs. Broker favored, granting them more recognition or praise than the pretty girls, or any of the boys.

Recess in those days, only boys took to the softball diamond or dodgeball courts. The girls just stood in semi-circles and talked, the better-looking ones keeping their distance from the less attractive ones. For the boys, it was a time of glory for the coordinated and fast, an occasion of humility for the slow, the clumsy, and the overweight, with Ed and Bryce among the underachievers, Ed because of his weight and lack of skills, and Bryce because he could not exert himself or deal with any pain, as he might while playing "bombardier," as the game was known there in Mesa.

Bombardier was like dodgeball, with the boys splitting into even numbers on opposite sides of a court. Each side took one soft, red rubber ball, and the object was to get your opponent "out," either by hitting him with the ball you threw or catching his. Ed was such a big target, he usually got hit early on, or dropped the ball he should have caught, and was eliminated early. Bryce simply avoided any contact with the ball until he happened to get hit, also in the early stages. And then there was Dale—always the last man standing, so swift, so smooth, so confident— he rarely missed, and his lithe body, which he moved with instinct and accuracy, no easy mark. He was, without question, the school's finest athlete, and he knew it. Perhaps that alone could make him the Alpha male, coupled with his bravado.

Thus, one day, just as the boys filed out onto the bombardier court, Dale held in his hand one red rubber ball and, on the opposite side, stood Ed, overweight, uncoordinated and usually one of the first out, with his rubber ball at the ready. The game had only barely begun, seconds really, when Ed made no move except to toss out his ball with a flick of the wrist, and it bounced off the top of Dale's foot. Dale stood still a few seconds, his mouth agape, shocked by the realization of what had just happened, and then silently plodded off the court, taking a place in the side lines, eliminated from the game immediately by, of all people, the class "ortho." All the boys laughed uproariously, and Dale managed a confused smile. Dale proved a good sport, and even congratulated Ed on a good game later, a milestone for someone so egotistical.

The months rolled by, the last year of elementary school before the harsh transition to junior high, when about three-fourths of the class would go on to Adams and the smaller group to Evans, a tad farther away, and more in the comfortable suburbs, rather than central Mesa. Mrs. Broker wore on them, but graduation approached. That included an award assembly and something of a summation of the year, which included song dedications which the members of the class made to each other. The students were arranged with half of the desks on one side of the room, and the other half facing them. Ed sat at the far end, near the semi-enclosed coat racks, and his friend Bryce facing toward him. They shared some laughs at the dedications.

"To Dale, from the girls in the class—'Leader of the Pack.'" That surprised no one, especially Dale. The biggest laugh came for Scott Sickles—"To Scott, alias Scot Tissue, 'Wipe Out!'" The dedications went on, some friendly, some good-natured insults, when it came time for one that caused some laughter and raised some eyebrows—"To Ed, from Bryce, 'I Want to Hold Your Hand.'"

Ed jumped up in surprise and, making the most of the occasion, dove into the coat rack area, pretending to be hiding from Bryce. The class roared, and Ed chewed over how to breach the subject with his friend later.

At the midday break, he addressed Bryce in a voice that he had toned down, but still carried incredulity.

"Bryce, *why* did you dedicate that song to me?"

"Oh, I don't know, it was all I could think of, and there was some pressure, so . . . " Bryce just spoke in his lilting voice.

Ed let it go, but he could never tell if Bryce had meant it as an attempt at humor or what deeper intimations may have been underlying. He went on next September to Evans Junior High, and Bryce to Adams, so the two never saw each other again until they ended up at the same high school, with an enrollment of over three thousand. They never had a class together and never spoke, though they saw each other from a distance. Ed observed how his old friend, now prominent in the drama scene, had developed an even softer tone of voice and more fainthearted gestures. Ed went on to become a teacher, and Bryce a professional actor and dancer, but their lives would cross again in the future, though neither could have foreseen how.

7

Travis in Phoenix.

T HE RIDE WITH Walt proved productive and smooth. Walt had been an actor earlier in his life, with a few bit parts on TV series and movies, making Travis envious, and then finally a more secure life teaching high school drama. With his almost musical cadence of speaking, Travis found himself intrigued by his new friend, and listened up as Walt proposed a solution to Travis's predicament.

"I have a lovely guest house in my backyard. A room with a mini-fridge, microwave, television, and VCR, very comfortable. You can stay there as long as you wish, if you are in doubt about lodging, which I highly suspect you are."

Sure, Travis could go along with that. He knew exactly what the pudgy teacher expected in return, but it sounded like a much better deal than anything he could find on the streets, especially a new town he knew nothing about. His own room? He had never had one, let alone with food and entertainment, at no cost. This would be the best deal ever.

A taxi took them to a suburb, with tree-lined streets and houses with neat lawns, several cuts above any place Travis had ever lived. Walt showed him his new digs, and it was bigger and cleaner than he had pictured. Sure enough, a good-sized TV and a VCR machine underneath a console, stocked with plenty of VHS tapes.

"You can also rent whatever tickles your fancy—just let me know ahead of time. I leave for work about six forty-five, home around four most afternoons, except when I need to stay late for my theater students, which is fairly often. Please don't go into the main house—I like to keep my privacy."

Travis just smiled and nodded his head, still wondering about this new stroke of luck. Was it too good to be true? Would all this be taken away from him soon? He figured he could hit Walt up for a little cash now and then, not too forcibly, so he could get some good grass and pills, maybe hustle, if he had to, during the day.

This was the easiest time of his short life. Walt would drop by for the evening, have his moments with Travis, and sometimes would just sit and pass the time. He told Travis stories about his career in theater, experiences he had had, and plenty of jokes. No street hustling, no sleeping in smelly hotels, just taking it slow and having lots of time to himself.

It was a week or so later that Travis overheard Walt talking over the telephone and saying things that did not add up, at first.

"Oh yes . . . let me explain. You see, he's my adopted son. Yes, there were these two dear friends of mine in LA, and they were involved in a terrible car crash, and they were both killed!"

Travis could not see Walt, but pictured his animated gestures and expressions that would match the dramatic pitch of his voice. He figured that Walt was the type who believed that if you said something loud enough, or with lots of gusto, people would believe it—something that was usually true. He listened on.

"And so they had no family nearby, and I felt the honorable thing to do was to take in this young man, and do my part. Yes, I will make sure he is enrolled in school soon."

That last sentence was a lie, like the others, and Travis knew it. He was just going to sit tight, enjoy this easy life—the "life of Riley," he had heard someone say; no work, just loafing around and being Walt's toy. "If it ain't broke, don't fix it," he had heard so many times, and this was just such a setting.

Weeks passed, and Travis ventured out to the suburbs, finding video arcades, movie theaters, and decent lunch hangouts where he spent Walt's money on whatever he felt like. His favorite lunch spot was a sandwich shop where the sandwiches took their names from local high school sports teams, including "the Lancer," "the Bruin," and "the Panther." Travis was determined to try each and every one of them, since he had all the time and money to do just that.

He was seated at a table alone, munching on a "jackrabbit," a mixture of many meats and cheeses, when he looked up at the TV in the diner, showing the afternoon news. Never one to follow the news, he barely glanced at the screen and almost yelled out, "Hey! That's Walt!"

Sure enough, there was his meal ticket being ushered off with his hands cuffed behind his back, two beefy cops leading him through glass doors, while reporters shoved microphones in his face. Walt kept his head down, looking ashamed and evasive.

The announcer's voice, same as all TV voices, spoke, "Charges brought against a local high school theater teacher and coach. Six separate counts of . . . "

There were some big words Travis did not know, but figured out what they most likely were.

"Homosexual relationships with three different male students . . . "

His home! That soft, easy life—he did not dare to return, because he knew the cops would be all over. If they questioned him, found out he was a minor, it would mean his return to Owensboro, back to the custody of his foster parents, a town still mad at him for his petty crimes.

There was just one choice: to cut and run. Take off, find a new place. Inside his pockets was just enough money from Walt to last a few days, then start hustling the lavender parts of Phoenix, wherever they were, and start making a living. Hollywood was just a bad dream, anyhow.

So it was back on the streets again. Travis headed into downtown Phoenix, meandering, getting acquainted with the streets and their characters. It was on one afternoon when a stranger approached him and muttered some words that were not intelligible, heavily muffled by some speech defect, and then handed Travis a card. All he could think of was that the stranger was asking for directions to the place on the card—"Hotel Aberdeen, 1221 Fifth Street." Knowing the general vicinity somewhat, Travis turned around, pointed to his right, and told the guy with the ragged speech about where the hotel would be. The stranger nodded, as if he already knew where it was and spoke again, just barely clear enough to understand:

"Whayya doin' tonigh'?"

Travis then realized what the stranger meant—this was a queer, looking for someone to join him and others, probably, for a get-to-gether, just for the fun. But if it was a known queer hangout, there were probably some visitors willing to put out some bucks for a big young stud. He told his brief acquaintance he was not interested, but later made tracks for what he hoped would be the source of some income. How else would he survive until the day he did make it in the movies?

The Aberdeen looked about how Travis had anticipated, an old building like so many you see in downtown anyplace, with a faded sign announcing its name, a sign which had probably been hanging there since long before Travis had been born. Sure enough, lots of scroungy looking characters stood idly by, all male, mostly young. He checked in, to a clerk at the counter who wore a sleeveless under-shirt and spoke behind crooked, smoke-stained teeth.

"Third floor, turn right. Pay for tomorrow, or check out early."

Travis paid for two nights and walked down the seedy hall-way on a dirty and worn carpet and hoped to pick up some extra cash, hustling the old homos who valued his company. But first, rub elbows with the locals and get to know the territory. He could just wander a ways, seek out the seedy sections, and then see what new sources he could find.

The room was much like the old shithole in Hollywood, what-ever its name had been, but smelled worse and cost less. He could hear partying at night and voices in the hallways, always male. He lounged and tried to sleep and longed for the comfort of Walt's guest-house, a vision that seemed so far back, though only a few days.

"I'll make more money, have things my way," he pledged to himself.

8

Travis and Bryce

THE STREETS OF Phoenix were hot, dirty, and teeming with all sorts of misplaced people. Normal, compared to Hollywood, but what place wouldn't be? It was on one afternoon that he encountered someone who was, in many ways, his exact opposite, but then again, similar. While strolling the soiled sidewalks, he saw someone, average height, maybe ten years or so older than himself, very mild in appearance and voice. Out in front of an adults only theater, the stranger spoke to Travis in a friendly and animated tone.

"My, aren't you the big one! Bet you feel safe in any neighborhood!"

Travis was leery by nature, but knew the soft-spoken man posed no threat—he could not be a cop in a million years, and held no ill intents. He was of slight build and carried himself with a body language that signaled gentleness, maybe even submission.

They spoke, off and on, with Travis mostly just listening and nodding, when a hooker in a leather miniskirt and halter top strutted by, looking more ridiculous than provocative. Travis gave her a good look over while his new friend just smiled, then said, "If her skirt were any shorter, she'd be wearing lipstick in *two-o-o-o* different places!"

Travis laughed out loud, hard and heavy for the first time in a long stretch, and decided he liked the new guy, as different as he may be.

"You sure were checking her out. I was wondering if you were one of us, you know, at this hang out," his new friend noted.

"Well, I still like girls better, but, gotta make money somehow. I guess you know how that goes," Travis told him.

"Oh yes, 'Gay for Pay,' as they say!" He spoke these words like others, with a flair and a slight twirl in his stance.

"Yeah, that's about it. Hoped to make it in the movies, no luck."

The stranger nodded in affirmation. "That's for sure. I am an actor, been in many plays in high school and local theaters, but never could make much of a living, being mostly a hoofer."

"'Hoofer'?"

"Oh, that's showbiz slang for a dancer. That's what I was best at. My name is Bryce, and you are?"

"Travis. Good to know you."

The gentle friend treated Travis to some iced coffee from a local stand, where the girl behind the counter thought to herself, *If there ever was a Mutt and Jeff routine, it's these two.* One was strikingly handsome, with wire glasses, and well-dressed—she kept her eyes on him. Only when she heard his singsong voice and saw the effeminate gestures, she knew he was a dead end for her. The other was bigger than life, with a tough expression and punk mohawk haircut, muscular and athletic looking. They took their drinks outside, continued their conversation, with Travis well engaged, until he told Bryce he needed to go back into the coffee shop for a pit stop.

Now alone, Bryce looked around worriedly and saw, with his peripheral vision, a hard, black face, maybe someone looking for trouble, so he looked askance, and tried to seem occupied. Bryce's first line of defense was always avoidance—just keep your distance from anyone who seemed threatening.

Like a shark cruising in the water, the predator spotted his mark, someone he could shake down for some bucks—no weapon, just intimidation. This was a queer place, and they preferred to surrender rather than resist. He targeted his next victim, soft and vulnerable, trying to look away from him, and he could smell the fear coming off the pretty white boy. Give him the snake eye, stare him down, he thought to himself.

He positioned himself directly in front of Bryce, who was seated and still trying to avoid eye contact. Not knowing what else to do, Bryce smiled, hoping a look of friendliness would spare him the bullying he had known for so many years. He had been the focus of tough black kids back in Mesa, though he was never sure if that was because of his pale skin or limp wrist, or maybe both. The smile did not work; he heard the loud ghetto voice yelling at him, nonstop and thunderous, wondering how to get out of this—he could not fight, so . . . appeasement?

"Ah tell you something, fairy-boy," pointing his black finger in his victim's face. Ah tell you, white bitch, what I'm about." The words grew louder, harsher, and caught the attention of passersby. The intimidator would not stop, screaming into Bryce's scared face, relentless, causing Bryce to draw back, trying to squirm away, as the yelling continued.

From the back of him, the aggressor heard a deep voice. "How 'bout you go back to yo' stand, and shine some shoes, *burr*-head?"

What the hell? This ain't Georgia, he thought. How many were standing behind him? His street-smart ears detected the confidence, with a trace of the South in the voice, low and almost a growl. Slowly, he turned to face his challenge.

He thought to himself, *Damn—just one of them, but look at him! Where did he get the guts?* Big, for sure, taller and stouter than himself, with menacing jailhouse tattoos. *I can get him to back off, cuz he's still just one white guy.* He looked hard and addressed the big punker with a confident tone.

"You caint talk to me like that and getta way wit' it, Honky."

"I just did. An' if you want to do somethin' 'bout it"—Travis tapped the back heel of his steel-toed boots on the curb—"I'll just put these boots up your black ass and through them *biiig*, thick lips o' yours. 'Cept I couldn't standa see a grown nigger cry."

The predator lowered his head, hoping to bluff the punker. He looked square at the face, saw how self-assured he seemed, saw the scars that showed the hits he had taken, the cockiness that showed he had dealt out worse, and the hard eyes of the redneck. He raised up his elbows and advanced with all the toughness he could muster. He got within a few feet of Travis before reality hit him—the big white kid wasn't flinching. Looking as if he had just run into a glass partition, he seemed to bounce backward and retreated. Looking over his shoulder, he made his parting shot. "Dumb ass, pecker wood faggots."

Bryce was still shaking, mostly from the confrontation, but partly from the raw racism he had just witnessed. Over the years, he had rejected the prejudice of his elders and never spoke the N-word, but he breathed deeply and tried to calm down, and addressed Travis.

"Um, thank you . . . he sure was frightening."

"You gotta show them you're not scared—get right in their face. The only way."

The two unlikely comrades sat and talked for a while, and Travis spoke of his youth, describing Owensboro and, among other things, the lightning bugs of Kentucky.

Bryce interjected, "Oh, you mean fireflies. I saw them for the first time with my dance troupe when we traveled back East. I had a friend who lived in Kentucky for a few years, the big town . . . "

"Lou-ah-ville," Travis told him.

"Yes, he said that's how they pronounce it back there. And how what folks in the Northeast call fireflies they call 'lightning bugs.' Instead of saying 'grandma and grandpa' . . . "

"Ma-maw and Pa-paw. Yep, that's what they're called." Travis felt relaxed and comfortable, a feeling he had not enjoyed in the last few weeks.

"So, Travis, if you don't mind, perhaps I could give you some direction. This is a somewhat decadent area, but nearby is what we call 'Lavender Lane' instead of 'Lovers' Lane.' At the heart of it is an upscale eatery called Sooner Burgers. You'll see a big sign with an outline of the map of Oklahoma. You know how Oklahoma is the Sooner State?"

No, Travis did not know that, and wondered what the map sign would look like, but he listened on . . . maybe this would lead him to someone like Walt, who would provide him with a steady place to stay.

"So just wander over there, look lost, and seek out the more expensive cars, and you'll probably find just the right one for you, a regular sugar daddy, and not have to work the streets."

After some more friendly talk, the two parted, agreeing to touch bases now and then, Bryce returning to his home and Travis to the Aberdeen. All night Travis dreamed of getting out of his stinky room and into the care of one of those older types Bryce had mentioned, maybe somehow still make it in the movies. Another Walt, another cozy place to stay, no more hustling. Yeah . . . Sooner Burgers . . . his ticket out.

9

TRAVIS SLEPT IN the next day and found his way across town until he located the area Bryce had described. He spotted a burger joint, larger than average, with an enclosed area and tables arranged outside, for those who could handle the hot weather. The sign above said Sooner Burgers and had an outline that looked like a meat cleaver to Travis. That must have been the map Bryce had told him about. The smell of french fries filled the air and mellow music played over the speakers. He ordered a combo of a double burger, fries and iced tea with free refills. No doubt about it, the food was awesome, but not cheap, and Travis kept his eyes open for a new client. Clearly, not all of the customers were on the lookout—many just came for the food and music.

Every day, he would meet up with someone who, if nothing else, would pick up the tab for his meal, and others invited him up to a hotel room nearby for services, just enough money to help Travis pay his rent at the Aberdeen. At least he might be able to afford a little better place to stay, if income increased. He eyed the vehicles as they pulled up, looking for expensive sports cars and signs of wealth.

One afternoon, he sat outdoors with his feet up and saw a long, shiny American-made auto roll up and park, somewhat awkwardly, along the sidewalk. Whoever was driving that car had money but drove like a jerk, which made Travis think he may have found something. The driver behind the wheel was easily old enough to be his dad, maybe older, with glasses and a face that needed a shave. A slob, really, in a fancy car. He watched the man open the door of his fine car and head toward Sooner Burgers with the ease that showed he was familiar with the place, a hangout for him.

Travis decided to mosey up to this middle-aged customer and see if it could lead to anything. As always, he let his target speak first. He gazed at the menu overhead, feigned uncertainty, and hoped the nerdy stranger would engage him in small talk.

Finally, the sloppily dressed man turned and addressed Travis in a voice that sounded like a cross between a lisp and someone trying to sound like an old lady. "My, the prices are a bit steep, but I hear the burgers and fries are worth every penny."

Travis knew that was an ice breaker, maybe even an invitation. After a few more simple words, the man would offer to pay for Travis's order, invite him to sit with him, and then work on luring him someplace private. All those hunches turned out to be correct.

Sure enough, within minutes, the hustler and the hustled were sitting together in a booth, munching away on the specialty, the OK Burger, and downing plenty of sweet iced tea, just like Travis was used to back in Owensboro.

A few awkward moments passed, when finally, the shaggy-haired man put out his hand. "How thoughtless of me! I must introduce myself—Francis Mackey. But you can call me Mack, if you want. Lots of people do."

"Travis Kingman. Nice to meet you, Mack. You live around here?"

"Oh, sort of . . . I'm on, oh, a long vacation, you might say. I have an apartment nearby. Maybe you'd like to stop by and we can watch some TV or something," Mack said, his voice softening.

They all started off like that—"or something." A hint. Travis only hoped that his latest contact in the big flashy car had some money and could offer him a better life. Maybe Mack could set him up the way Walt had, and just take life easy, without any street hustling, or wondering about how he might eat or where to sleep, freedom from the seedy Aberdeen.

Mackey continued the discourse. "So where from, stranger? Not around here, I can tell by your accent. I bet you're a transplant, as am I."

"Owensboro, Kentucky. Downriver from Louisville a ways. You come from up North some place?" Travis knew to keep the conversation rolling, win the trust of the older man.

"Minnesota—out of the ice box and into the oven, you might say. Had to get away from those frozen winters. Now I bake all year. But at least there's no snow to shovel and ice on the roads around here. In Phoenix, they put on coats if its gets under seventy. Say, I'll be dropping by here for lunch on Tuesday, if you would want to get together and chat some more." He followed these words with a light, "hmmm," making Travis wonder what path Mackey would take next.

Travis nodded his head and smiled, not sure why his new contact did not want to speed into a hotel or bathroom the way it often went. The two new acquaintances said goodbye, and Travis sat still, watching the peculiar guy head to his big car, get in, and pull away after a few hesitant attempts to merge with traffic.

After two lunch dates, Travis finally got invited to Mackey's apartment. It was small, a contradiction to the sort of car Mackey drove, but Travis knew that soon the older man would be offering him money or gifts in exchange for sexual favors. All that happened, but not in the usual manner. Mackey had no drugs, maybe because he was such a square, and usually just handed out soft drinks, with an occasional beer, but the talk turned to cash soon. And instead of sex, Mackey wanted Travis to perform for him on camera. From a cardboard box, Mackey extracted a movie camera, with an opening for VHS tapes, something still fairly new at the time, and had Travis act out situations—undressing, showering, and, what appealed most to Mackey, variations of Travis playing with himself. The tapes did not need to be taken anywhere, just ready to go, a fairly recent development, and the still photos were the type that just popped out instantly. So there was no danger of outsiders learning of the shootings. As long as the dollars kept coming, and they did, Travis was partly satisfied, but tried to think of a way to milk Mackey for more.

Travis wondered what Mackey did with the tapes; probably just watched them in his spare time, or maybe entertained friends with them, if Mackey had any friends. That was hard to tell, since Mackey rarely spoke of his private life—what he did for a living, for example. But one evening, with his benefactor busy in the kitchen, Travis snooped a bit and found some envelopes with no markings. He carefully opened one of them and found dozens of photographs, all basically the same—young guys jacking off, showing off what they had, and looking ridiculous. How old were they? His age? Some looked younger. Most people assumed Travis was twenty or so, maybe because his time in juvie had hardened him. He slid the photos back into the envelope and returned it to its original spot, hoping Mackey would not notice.

Weeks passed, and Mackey kept the money flowing, easy enough and not bad, so that Travis could keep his room and buy a few joints, along with his basic needs. Whenever Travis tried to squeeze him for more cash, Mackey would take on his maternal voice and say, "Now, now, my boy, that should hold you a spell." Travis noted that Mackey never allowed him to spend the night and was probably not the type to mention his relationship with Travis to anyone. Mackey never told Travis his occupation or where his work was, either. Careful, he guessed, something Walt should have done, and avoided prison. Travis did not know for sure what became of Walt but judged that he had to do at least some time for his crimes, and for sure lost his job forever.

One evening, Travis was over at Mackey's apartment, sitting in the small living room while Mackey mixed up some ice cream soda treats, taking his time and humming as he did it. Over on a stand next to the sofa where Travis sat lay a pile of unopened mail. Bills, ads, nothing interesting until one label provided him with some answer to the mystery that Travis had been puzzling over. There, on the front of a magazine, it read, "Dr. F.D. Mackey." Huh? *Doctor*? He never would have guessed the scroungy-looking slob to have been a doctor. He did not resemble the doctors Travis had seen on TV shows, square types in white coats who came home to a big white house in the suburbs to a gorgeous wife and cute kids, or even as clean-cut as the medics who had treated him for drug addiction and clap at the public clinics. He chewed on his new discovery and kept it to himself for pondering.

Back in his hotel room, Travis stared up at the ceiling, examining the cracks and stains, and knew he needed a brighter future. It looked like the movies either weren't going to come through, or he would have to put it off for the future. How could he get a hold of some money, enough to live better, maybe get an apartment, buy a car, when he turned eighteen in a few months? That made him sit up—not eighteen? *I'm still a minor. Does Mack know or suspect that?* He thought about Walt, whose career was shattered, and his future forfeited when the truth came out about the underage teens he had fiddled around with. What was it that cop said to him, just as he got ran out of Hollywood? He was after the older guys that he could put in jail? If Mackey were a doctor, he would have a lot of money, and going to jail, along with the public disgrace, would be so harmful that he would be willing to hand over some of it to Travis to get him out of his life. Travis was skeptical, but would work up his courage, pressure Mackey for a big chunk of cash, and then move up in his life. The hell with the Aberdeen and these old homos.

10

T HE NEXT MORNING, Travis sat at a local coffee shop, munching bagels and trying to figure out how to put the pinch on Mack. He knew enough, from the trouble he had been in, that usually the police needed some evidence past just anyone's say-so to put a criminal away. Fingerprints, the word of witnesses, and pictures. Yeah, pictures! He thought of the camera he had swiped from his family before he ran off, a fairly decent one, and he could use that. But how could he take pictures of him and Mack doing anything without his target knowing? Travis started putting together a subtle way of approaching the doctor and knew, however educated Mack was, he was not street smart enough, did not have the instincts, to realize what was happening.

Back in his room, he found the camera in a compartment in his backpack and sat back to rehearse his approach. He would assume a mild tone, maybe even a bit of a sad one, and play on some sympathy. He would be careful not to come on too strong, just gently get into the apartment, manage a few pictures to prove that he, a minor, and Mackey, an adult, were in an illegal relationship. Then he could simply tell Mackey, give me the money (he was not sure how much to ask for) and I go away forever. Don't, and its jail, and your career goes down the toilet. Simple enough.

A few days later, Travis met Mack for lunch and ended up at his apartment as usual. While Mack was in the can, Travis whipped out his camera, loaded with a roll for thirty-six exposures, and snapped shots of the inside of the apartment and some mail with Mackey's name and address on it. He waited for Mack to emerge, and then assumed his softer voice.

"Say, Mack, you know how I told you I'm still trying to make it in the movies? I gotta lead, and they want some photos. Could you take a few for me?"

"Well, of course, my friend. Hope they do the trick. I'm something of a shutterbug, so let me give it a try. Strike one of those sensuous poses you're noted for."

Travis sat for an ordinary picture, then stood and flexed his large and leathery muscles for another shot. Feigning hesitation, he pulled off his tank top and revealed his well-developed pecs and abs. Eventually, he removed all of his clothes and posed nude.

"Just in case they want to go X-rated," he told Mackey.

"Oh yes, this should sell you well to your prospects," Mackey responded.

Later, after sipping some iced tea and munching cookies, Travis brought up the next question as if it had just popped into his head.

"Oh, I just thought of something. My folks back in Owensboro are worried I have no friends out here. Would you mind helping fix that? A picture of the two of us, hanging out? The camera has a timer, so I can set it, plop next to you on the couch, and then—ZING!"

"Sure, and then you need to head off. Got some big plans for tomorrow, and then we can get together in a week or so."

Travis set the camera upright on a counter, raced over to sit next to his victim, and tried to make them look like lovers. The camera flashed, made a whirring noise, and Travis knew that his plan was about to roll. Mackey must have been well-educated, but no clue of the grave mistake he had just made, allowing evidence of a crime in commission. Of course, this may have been because Mackey was not fully aware that what he was doing was illegal, since Travis's minor-age status was still a secret.

They said goodnight, and Travis dreamed of how he would make his next move. He dropped into a drug store, put the roll of film in a packet, and wrote Mackey's name and address, which he had copied off the mailbox, on the label. That would leave more of a trail to the scroungy loser. He checked the box requesting doubles, noted the due date, and found his way down the dark sidewalks back to the Aberdeen.

He sat in the lobby, watching old TV shows with the regulars, but not engaging in any conversation. His mind was preoccupied with his plan, and it filled him with both nervous anxiety and hopeful excitement. How much should he demand from Mack? Too much, and the old timer would at least balk, but enough to help Travis get a new life, so . . . fifty-thousand seemed doable. Mackey probably had about that much in savings, or could take out a loan since he had a fine car and said he had a big house elsewhere, though Travis had never seen it and figured he never would. Yeah, fifty grand, all in cash, so he could find some place better, a used car, and treat himself until he got that break in the movies, or at least some occupation, once he was eighteen.

He returned to his room and thought of nothing but his scheme. He knew someone as wussy as Mack would be scared shitless by one night in a county jail, so hard time in a real prison would be something he could never consider. How would he confront Mackey? Come across as strong, show he meant business, and not bluffing, same way he made others back down from a fight—they'd take the easier way out, rather than deal with a tough guy. Just wait, and old Travis was going to be getting by much better in life.

Their next get-together followed a week afterwards. Mackey taped Travis in various nude or semi-nude activities, and sometimes they just sat and talked, with Mackey doing most of the talking, and Travis just nodding his head, pretending to be interested, getting his target to relax. Using a casual tone, he asked, "How 'bout if we drop by that corner store and pick up a few things? Got the munchies, maybe something to drink."

Mackey smiled blandly and got up from the kitchen table, getting his wallet out of a drawer, where he kept his keys and other pocket items. They walked quietly to the store Travis had indicated, and both sought out some snacks, with Travis hanging out in the front while Mackey perused drinks from the refrigerated area. Travis leaned over the counter, making conversation with the Korean clerk.

After a while, Travis introduced himself to the Asian, shook his hand, and engaged in more friendly talk. He found the surveillance camera, looked up at it deliberately and knew that he could count on the clerk and maybe the video as proof that he and Mack had been together, especially as he stalled next to him as Mack paid for their refreshments.

Back at the apartment, Travis took another measure. Remembering where Mack's photos were, he secretly slipped out two of the dozens of young guys posing nude. One he slipped into his backpack, another he hid on a bookshelf in Mack's living room. If Mackey feared arrest, he would destroy his collection, but the police would find the one Travis buried among Mackey's books. If need be, he could mention the hidden photo as part of the threat he could use against Mack. The pieces were beginning to fall into place.

After an hour or so of just munching and slurping, Travis said goodbye and left, hoping to give Mack a feeling of complacency. Travis continued to the drugstore, where he picked up the envelope of now-developed photos. Paying cash, he took his treasure to his room and sorted through them, making separate piles, one to pressure his victim with, and the other secreted away in a compartment in his backpack. He would hide the negatives somewhere else, not sure where for now, but his plan was starting to ripen. This was the most excitement he had felt in a long time, and he was bursting with the desire to tell someone, even though he hardly knew anyone in Phoenix besides the doctor and that fruitcake who told good jokes and had steered him toward Sooner Burgers. What was his name? Brian? No, Bryce, that was it. Maybe tomorrow, since he had some extra cash from Mackey, he would treat himself to some iced drinks where he had first met Bryce—most likely he would find his friend there.

11

AFTER A NIGHT of tossing, Travis got up, exercised vigorously as he did every day, several times a day, and headed down the dark sidewalks that led back to the scummy bookstores and movie theaters that attracted the forlorn. At a hot dog stand, he ordered some fries and iced tea, planted himself, and watched the world go by.

Not too much time passed before he heard a familiar voice ring out, and Travis looked up to see the lightly freckled face and glasses of his casual friend. Any friend seemed like a reprieve to Travis who, though he would never admit it, often felt lonely and deserted.

"Well look who's here, my bodyguard, my most ardent supporter, the Owensboro original in the flesh! How have things been for you, Travis?"

Travis responded with some happiness in his voice, "Not bad, not bad at all. Been to that high-class burger joint you described, found some old geezers who were willing to put out some cash. One for sure, he's a regular and, believe it or not, he's a doctor."

"Oh my, Travis, don't tell me the two of you have been *playing doctor*, at your age!" Bryce said this with a skipping motion, dancing in a circle, and waving his hands. Travis chuckled, and smiled once again, enjoying his time with one of the few pleasant people he had found. As he had thought before, two opposites, but similar in other ways.

After some more light talk, Travis decided to let Bryce in on his secret. He gathered up his thoughts and began to unload.

"There's some things about me I should tell you about, Bryce. Got to be just between the two of us, though."

"For sure, my lips are pursed, and I will be your confidante!"

Travis hesitated, then told him, "Not too many know this, but I'm still seventeen, at least for a few months."

"Oh, then it's a good thing we're just pals, nothing intimate, then. And that's how it must stay, since I'm thirty, baby face or not. Those clients must not know, and if they do, they could get into some big-time troubles. Maybe you need to go to a youth help outfit, something along those lines? For runaways, is that it?" Bryce asked, his tone sympathetic.

"Yeah, I took off to get away from foster parents and other crap, but I can't return, and one of those places might send me back. I'll hang on till I'm eighteen, and I have a plan for making myself much better off."

Bryce spoke up, trying to encourage him. "If you're thinking of some sort of decent job, that might work out. You'll get minimum wage, but if that's all you can handle, wait to move up as time passes, that's how I have been. Much of my acting has been at places that did not pay at all, so there have been rinky-dink jobs for me, even though I graduated from college. Of course, I've lived with my folks for much of that time, been lucky."

Travis sounded cocky as he told Bryce, "Better than that, I got a plan to get some money out of him—lots. When I tell him I'm still a minor, I'll say 'I'll go to the cops,' and he'll pay up. That or he could go to prison, lose his license, stuff like that. I can tell he's the type to take the easy way out and just pay me."

"Oh, Travis, you can't mean extortion?"

"Ex . . . tor . . . tion?" Travis's eyes narrowed at the unknown word.

"Yes, you know . . . blackmail. It's a serious offense, not like weed or soliciting, where you can get off easy. I got caught soliciting once, did some community service for a few weekends, and then—*poof*—it went away. But this is terrible. You can go to prison and, big and tough and strong as you may be, there are brutes in there who will ravish you, nonstop, and the violence against gays is beyond

53

your worst dreams. You may have heard the old jokes about how in the shower room, you have to keep turning around? Travis, I implore you, *don't!*"

Travis guessed that *implore* meant *beg* and returned to his thoughts. What Bryce had just said all made sense, but he knew he had to get out of this circle he was in, find an easier life, and he felt confident he could pull it all off—he knew how to control the weak like Mackey, and a fat envelope of cash would be his ticket to a new town, a new life, and a future for once.

Bryce and Travis spoke briefly, with Travis trying to change the subject, but Bryce could only hope he had planted enough doubt into his young friend's mind not to follow through with his intentions. After some uncomfortable milling around, Travis rose up, said good-bye to his only companion, and made his way back to the Aberdeen, his heart and mind heavy with his dark plan.

12

TRAVIS PACED AROUND the outside of Mackey's apartment. The rundown neighborhood seemed depressing, but maybe that would help him follow through with his mission. He thought about all the fights he had been in—*Show your nerve, make sure the other guy knows you will not back down, so he will have to. Show any hesitation, things will go south.* He clutched the envelopes with the photos in one hand and walked, with resolve, to Mackey's door.

Like always, Mack opened the door with a lopsided smile and gestured for Travis to enter. "Do come in. How about a drink?" he offered, casually.

Travis shook his head, remained silent, and kept a serious look on his face. This was the moment, he knew, push his advantage, and leave no room for bargaining. Go one way or the other, he had always learned—put up a fight or get the hell out, but don't mess with anything between.

As they stood there, a bit awkwardly, Mackey gabbed a bit about his current affairs, when Travis blurted out his threat.

"All right, doctor, this is it," he said in a deep and confident tone, and handed Mackey the envelope. "You know what those are, you took them. Anyone can see they were taken in your place, and we're together in one of them. More than that, I swiped two of those pictures of your other boys. I got one, and another is here in your apartment, but you probably won't find it before the cops do."

Cops? Mackey scratched the stubble of his scraggly whiskers and felt genuine fear. He had been careful, he thought, in the past.

55

High school teachers could be fired and jailed for taking liberties, but in college, as long as you were not exacting favors in exchange for grades, nothing happened. Besides, Travis was not a student, so what did this young punker think he could pressure him with?

"That's right, *Doctor* Mackey, you could lose everything. Even if you get away with it with the law, you know it means your career goes down the toilet, right, *Doctor?*" Travis pressed on.

Why is he calling me "doctor," Mackey thought, *especially with that inflection? Years ago, people got arrested just for being homosexual, but that was fading into the past, now into the eighties. This uneducated fool must think he had enough on him to cause trouble.*

Travis turned up the assertive tone and volume in his voice. "And you know something, *Doctor?* I'm still seventeen—you didn't know that! Yep, born *almost* eighteen years ago, but still a minor for a few months. That means what we have been doing is a crime, and you can do time for it, plus losing your job forever.

"So it's easy. One, you hand me fifty thousand dollars, cash, in an envelope, and I take off, you never see me again, everything's all right. You hold back, I go to the cops, they'll be all over this place and the house where you live, where you work, it will be in the news, and no turning back. I'll be back in a week, you hand over the money, and that's all!"

Travis turned, stomped out the door, slamming it on the way out, and left Mackey standing in his foyer, dumbfounded and shaken.

This was real, but seemed unreal. Mackey had estimated Travis to be about nineteen or a bit older, not a minor like some of the other boys he had found in other locations. He had always heard that if you do anything illegal, improper, or anything that might get you in trouble, eventually you will get caught, no matter how careful you may be. Then, it all comes down on you, and you have to deal with the consequences—the punishment, the embarrassment, and the shame.

Prison? Mackey had never been strong or tough in his youth, often picked on by schoolyard bullies and street hoodlums, but at sixty, he knew he would be the daily treat for all those monsters behind bars. Could he beat the rap? He could say Travis lied about his age, used a fake ID, and maybe, with a good lawyer, enough doubt would be raised to get him off. But he could lose his teaching position, maybe also his pension, and he had never saved much money for retirement. No pension! Could he live off social security alone?

Pay Travis that fifty grand? He would have to borrow it, since he had spent a fortune keeping his parents in a convalescent home the last few years of their lives. Giving in seemed like the best alternative, the easy way out, but he knew of too many extortion cases that never ended. The blackmailer would come back, squeeze the victim for more, even years afterwards, and that could drive him into poverty. A kid like Travis would most likely blab about what he was doing, and that meant the police would come after him one day.

And Travis had said he had acquired one of the photos of his young cohorts, but there was no way of proving the boy in the picture was under or over eighteen—Mackey was never quite sure himself. The police would search all his property and office, like Travis had indicated, and that alone disturbed him deeply. He quickly gathered all incriminating pictures, the ones Travis had handed him, as well as a few dozen of his former customers, took them into the bathroom and lighted each on fire with lighter, dropping the ashes into the toilet bowl, and flushing.

He could think of nothing except the threat. He did not have one moment of peace or focus. He anguished, gnashing his teeth, shaking his head, and trying to breathe normally, but could not. His face felt hot, and he clenched and unclenched his fists continuously. Like everyone else, Mackey had had his worries over the years, but nothing like this—the publicity, the guilt, maybe going to prison. He felt relieved that his parents had passed on just a few years ago, and wondered about his brother, a priest in New Haven. That little brother had looked up to him, bragged about Mack's college teachings and publications, and Mack dreaded how deflated he would feel.

By the end of the day, he had come to a conclusion, a conclusion he had never dreamed possible, of something so far out of the range of the pusillanimous professor's character, but what he felt was the only solution.

Travis had no family in Phoenix, he had said. There was no one here to notice if he disappeared. So Travis was going to disappear.

13

MACKEY KNEW VERY little about guns, a city guy, never an outdoors man, and a long-time supporter of the strictest gun control laws. He had railed against the Second Amendment for years in his classroom and every opportunity he had. Thus he felt awkward, to put it mildly, entering a gun store with right-wing posters all over, bumper stickers about how guns made America free, and customers who looked either like cowboys or blue-collar toughs. Out of place, he collected his courage and waited for a chance to approach the counter when it was not busy.

The employee was, by far, the prettiest male Mackey had ever seen in his life. His long hair and gentle blue eyes made him think of the portraits of Jesus he had seen in his missal as a Catholic child and he thought to himself, *Even straight guys could not take their eyes off him.* At the same time, he saw something completely contradictory to the clerk's appearance—a large pistol on his hip, like the ones Mackey had seen in westerns from his childhood. With some reserve, he spoke to the clerk in a hesitant voice.

"Could you give me some pointers about which gun I should purchase? You might say I'm new at this."

"Sure thing, pardner. You say you're a beginner, so you probably want a revolver—takes a little less practice and generally considered safer. Except for cleaning, maybe easier to maintain." He reached down below the counter and retrieved a pistol significantly smaller than the one on his belt and gingerly pointed the gun downward, moved something with his thumb, and the cylinder rocked outward.

"This is a .38," he told Mackey, confidently. "Not too much of a kick, easy to carry and use. Not the same stopping power as a .45, but you don't always need that. Bullets go in here, fires six. Reloading takes practice, but speed loaders can help. Seen cops reload in seconds, but they've had plenty of practice."

Mackey nodded to show he was paying attention. He asked about the price and any accessories. He remembered from movies that the shells in a revolver stayed in the gun, not ejecting like others, so that made the .38 more attractive. He would not have to worry about spent shells that may not get picked up.

The beautiful clerk quoted the price and told him how he could buy a package that included a cleaning kit and extra boxes of ammo at a discount. Mackey rummaged through his pockets, found the cash he had brought from his closet, and paid up. After having the clerk show him how to load and unload again, he thanked him and took the package, careful not to reveal the contents to anyone, and exiting as if he had just committed a crime.

He drove, with nervous energy, to the college campus and walked to his office, which was empty late in the afternoon. He went through the cleaning devices, rolling the tiny rod around in his fingers, wondering what difference it would make. He would only use the gun once, then never see it again. He pushed the kit, wrapped up in a receipt, back behind some old term papers that he had graded but never read. He put the gun and case of bullets in a big brief case he had not used in years and headed back to his apartment.

He told himself, *Don't go to the house—leave no evidence there.* Then again, he may need to rid his house of the myriad of VHS tapes and pictures that were in his room with no furniture, where he had taped encounters with young guys and had hoped to continue, but this experience was causing him pause. The follow-up of clearing his house of any incriminating evidence would come later.

Mackey had made up his mind. He could do this; he knew how the law worked, he was an educated man, and he could think his way through this task. Otherwise, his future was doomed.

14

FOR THE NEXT few days, Mackey kept the pistol close at hand, trying to get a comfortable feel for it so he could accomplish his task without hesitation. This made him feel like he was doing something so out of character, but it brought excitement, mingled with shades of guilt. He had worked up his resolve and plotted out how he would carry it through.

On the arm of his reading chair was a cloth holder, with compartments for his books, reading glasses, and pencils. He secreted the small gun near the top, memorized its exact location, and practiced retrieving it from its hiding place. Travis was strong, quick, and had sharp reflexes, so the only way to do this was to catch him unawares and fire without warning. No conversation or choice words, like he had seen in those gangster movies he had watched as a child in Minnesota. Just do it and move on.

Next chore was to get rid of the body. He knew of a secondhand luggage store that should carry what he needed to dispose of the carcass. He drove out there early in the day and found a large trunk, long and deep, and Mackey paid cash at the counter, making no eye contact with the clerk. The best feature was the small castors on the bottom, meaning he could roll the trunk out. He knew he would not be strong enough to lift anything too heavy, and this had to be a solo job.

Mackey paced nervously all day, and the next day, unable to think of anything but what he had to do. He felt anxious, wanting the act to be done and over with, almost hopeful. He figured that Travis, like always, would appear after dark, as he had done before. He would feign compliance, even submission, and wait for the golden opening where he could dispatch the young thug. As he had thought earlier, no one would miss him, or think to report anything. Whoever Travis knew would just assume he had jumped up and headed elsewhere, like he had done in the past. That family he had mentioned back in Kentucky would have no way of knowing that he dropped off the radar.

Two nights later, the dark moment arrived. When Travis appeared at the apartment, close to midnight, Mack let him in, mumbled softly, and motioned for him to be seated, but Travis remained on his feet. Travis carried himself with confidence, giving off an air of self-assurance, knowing that getting his way, like always, depended on pushing forward and not letting the other have any leeway. Mack kept his head down, not looking in Travis's direction, and wandered into the small living room. He placed himself near the easy chair with the hidden gun and tried to look downcast, which for the most part, he was. Travis rambled about how he knew that Mack had the cash, so why not get this over and done with, and . . .

In what seemed like slow motion, Travis saw the small handgun from his peripheral vision, thought of the snub-nose his Uncle Griff kept behind the counter at the gas station, and his gut instincts flared, turning to ward off the attack. He was not quite fast enough—the gun barked, hitting Travis in the ribs, causing searing pain and for him to stumble forward. He tried to spin around and hit Mack with his forearm, but Mackey barely dodged him, stepped behind the big youth, pushed the muzzle to the back of his head, and fired one more time.

Mack's neighbor arose partly from his sleep, wondering if he had just heard some shots or if his Vietnam memories were haunting him again, and . . . did he hear something heavy hit the floor? That was one weird character who lived upstairs, so who knew what he and some other pervert were doing. He rolled over and returned to his sleep.

Mack stared at the dead heap in front of him, thinking was it just a bad dream, or had he really done this? His heartbeat was

E. WAYNE CUNDIFF

accelerated, his jaw clenched shut, and he started to shake with emotion. If anyone heard anything, they would most likely assume it was gang activity, which there was plenty of around here. He knew that he must act expediently and follow up with the next stage of this crime—disposing of this corpse.

After sitting down in an effort to regain his composure, he rolled out the trunk and tried to lift the thick, muscular body, still warm. Mackey was not a strong man, never had been, but he gripped the arms and pushed up with both legs, using his knee to push the body upward, barely making it over the edge of the trunk, and using his left foot, pushed Travis's butt up. At this point, he realized a mistake.

He had misjudged the length of the trunk, and there was no way the long legs were going to fit. He could not possibly push it in, and the body would not be concealed. He sat down and tried to come up with a plan. A fan of old movies, he thought about a fifties flick that involved a reporter, sick in bed or something, looking out his window with binoculars and slowly coming to believe he was witnessing the aftermath of a homicide. A man who had just killed his wife was disposing of the parts, one by one, in various containers.

So that was it, he grimly thought. Rummaging through his kitchen, he found a cleaver left by his mother that she had used when chopping up chicken. He raised the cleaver, drew up his courage, and hacked once into Travis's brawny shoulder. He struck with all his might and knew that this would not work, no matter how hard and long he tried. He lacked the power, the finesse, or both. Would a saw work?

He had no tools, not a handyman by any means, so he decided there must be some better method. Meanwhile, what about the stiff, now cold, and soon to start rotting and smelling? He turned the air conditioner up full blast, too cold for anyone, and after a quick change of clothes, drove to a nearby twenty-four-hour store. The clerk looked a bit surprised to see someone buying twenty-pound bags of kitty litter in the wee hours but just took Mackey for one of those people who ran his errands at night for whatever reasons.

Back at the apartment, Mackey covered the corpse with the kitty litter and wrapped himself up in blankets, trying to sleep, which

62

did not come, except for brief naps as he turned restlessly, unable to rid his brain of the images of the victim, his contorted face as he fell, and the sounds of his dying breath.

Mackey knew of a rental place for moving vans not far from his home. Only a block or so from it was a long-term parking garage, where he placed his car, and then walked about three blocks to Homan's Haulers, an independent business that rented out vans and trucks. He engaged the clerk in straightforward talk and rented the smallest van available, figuring he could handle the steering. Before leaving, he bought packs of three different brands of cigarettes, remembering a trick from some novel he had read in the past, positioned himself behind the steering wheel and clumsily drove down the street.

Rhett Quincy had worked at the rental business a few years and mostly saw customers who were pretty much the same—middle-class guys who knew, more or less, what they were doing with the equipment they used for a day or two and then returned, the type who saved a buck by fixing things themselves, handy types, and the occasional fool who just thought he could take care of things around his house, but he had never seen anyone give off an aura of ineptness like the loser who wandered in just now. Leaning his elbows on the counter, he took a quick inventory: older than most, and with some nervousness that Rhett could not figure out. Something was bugging this jerk, but what?

Spastic—he and his chums had tossed that word around when he was a teenager (only a few years ago) to describe this sort. His questions revealed his lack of experience. Yes, the gas type was stronger, could cut through about anything, and here's how you start it . . . Well, that came with his job, but usually he felt the customer could handle the equipment—not sure about this one. He asked for some ID, took a picture of the shaky man with the instant camera, and processed his credit card for the deposit. He watched the sorry guy exit, and Rhett wondered what he might be up to, then returned to his paperwork.

Mackey had not expected to have his picture taken, and that made him worry, but too late now. That skinny young lad with the shaved head had been nice enough to him, but Mackey could tell he had been laughing up his sleeve. Rhett—what a name! Nothing like the fictional character, with his boyish face and dull eyes. With some effort, he carried his precious tool to the van, wrapped it up in canvas, propped himself up behind the wheel and headed back to his apartment, dreading the task ahead of him.

When Mackey returned to his apartment, he knocked on the doors of his neighbors, ready with an innocent question about if anyone had seen his nephew, in case someone answered, but no one did. Good—they were all at work, as he had hoped, and would not hear the chainsaw, which he had already secretly set down in the living room. He went back to his place, turned up the TV and radio, and set to work on dismembering the arms and legs, wearing a set of goggles he had purchased from the hardware store. He recalled, from his reading of history, how the first chainsaws invented were intended, not for lumber, but for amputating human limbs.

Mackey used linen from his closet to wrap up both arms in one sheet and both legs in the other. The head and torso remained in the trunk, now able to fit inside, exposing Travis's lifeless face, that seemed almost at peace for once. He dumped in some more litter and lime, hoping it would cover any odor, at least for a while, and then closed the lid and latched it. Looking around the room, he knew he would have to scrub down the carpet and walls later, though the splatter was not nearly as vast as he had imagined it would be. He knew he would have to wait for dark to move the remains, should anyone see bloodstains on the sheets.

His clothes, as well as those of Travis—no way could he keep them or let them be found. Everything went into a plastic garbage bag, doing the same with Kingman's jeans and shirt in a separate bag, along with the VHS tapes of Travis, and he showered to remove any traces, thinking of that old movie with the leading lady showering, symbolic of cleansing her conscience, only to meet death herself. He got dressed in a different set of clothes, gathered the plastic bags, and headed to the rented moving van. He knew a good dumping place—the back of a redneck bar that he knew to be hostile to his kind, a bar filled with cigarette smoke and loud country music, where the barflies said the word *fag* out loud, and no one winced. Pulling up in the alley, he heaved the bag and its contents into a dumpster. He looked at the dumpster a few moments, trying to grasp the reality of what he was doing, and slowly drove back to his apartment, waiting for nightfall.

15

A FTER DUSK FELL, Mackey prepared to carry out his next task. He parked the van close to his apartment door, with the back open, and a ramp lowered. The trunk scooted along the carpet slowly, then increased speed on the linoleum, out the front, down the stairs—a bit tricky—and up into the van. He looked around nervously, making sure no one had seen him, then went back to retrieve the other parts in the bedding sheets. This took two trips, but Mackey had all the remains of Travis inside the storage area of the van, closed the back, and returned to the bathroom, where the gun and wallet still lay. He folded them in a towel, and after locking up his apartment, drove out of town without a clear destination in mind, just to be in the dark countryside. Sighting an irrigation canal, he stopped, tossed in the towel, and continued on the interstate.

As he drove through the midnight miles, with the traffic thinning out, Mackey came to an interchange and noted the thick shrubbery around the on-ramps—good for cover, and no one would see him disposing of the limbs, or if they did, never think he was up to something as sinister as what it was. He pulled the van up close to the shrubs, opened up the back partly, and fetched the linens. Peering about, he waited for a quiet moment to drop off the parts and leave without drawing attention.

Rolling along that same interstate, trucker Gavin McKeevy, alias "The Commander," spoke on his CB radio, telling a litany of jokes with fellow gear jammers as he filled up the empty hours. Having obtained his handle from a TV show from his childhood, about a

cadet named McKeevy who was always at odds with the comman-
dant in charge of the academy, he was just finishing one of his longer
jokes, when he told the other truckers he needed to stop and "get
ahold of myself," as he liked to say.

McKeevy pulled his rig over, glanced at the siding with "Carpet
Corpsman" painted on it, and with the medical insignia he knew was
called a caduceus, something he had learned from Mr. King, his high
school Latin teacher. The owners of the rental cleaning equipment
had named the business "Carpet Corpsman" because they were Navy
vets, like his dad, and the name was accompanied by a cartoonish
Navy corpsman cleaning a rug. He headed off into the semi-secluded
area to relieve himself, when the quiet was interrupted by a roar, the
deep angry voice of a big man.

"What the hell you think you doin' on my property?"

McKeevy stammered, not thinking of an excuse quickly enough,
when the shadow accused him, "You came back here to take a *whizz*,
dintchoo? Well, just get back in your truck and go the hell some-
wheres else!"

He nodded, sheepishly returned to his truck, and began to pull
away, when he caught sight of something odd, maybe a hundred
yards into his retreat. He made out a moving van from a company
he had encountered occasionally over the years, "Homan Haulers,"
and the silhouette of a man, carrying bags in both arms, and headed
into the ivy not far from the on-ramp. Whoever he was looked over
his shoulder two or three times, in what looked like nervousness.
What in the world? He stopped, studied the hesitant figure for a
moment, noted what might have been a hairpiece, or odd hat, and
large glasses, and then rode on, looking for a rest area, but haunted
by what he had just seen, whatever it had been.

Mackey had no idea any one had observed him disposing of the
arms and legs, and got on the freeway, and headed into the more rural
areas. After maybe an hour of driving the moving van, still a challenge
for him, he pulled off near what looked like a ranch. Coyotes scur-
ried away from him, as he turned off the lights and pulled up near
a fence that served as the perimeter around a farm. He remembered
the smell, from his youth in Minnesota, but could not place it, some

crop, maybe alfalfa. With some effort, he rolled the trunk out of the back of the van, opened the lid, tipped it, and Travis's torso and head fell out, louder than what he had intended, though the area looked deserted. He pulled the trunk into the van, closed it, and got out the cigarettes. He lighted three of them, different brands, coughed harshly, then stamped them into the dirt, thinking to himself that the police would look for a trio of smokers, one habit Mackey had never developed. He felt almost cocky at his cleverness, when he heard an indiscernible noise from the distance. Panicking, he jumped back into the cab, drove off hastily, searching for a dumping place for the trunk. He drove about halfway back to Phoenix, pushed the trunk off an edge, where it landed among other piles of discarded household items, and continued on, his breathing and heartbeat irregular.

When Mack returned to his apartment, he tried scrubbing down the bathroom, carpet, and any areas where blood may have spattered. Sleep would not come easily, or steadily, but he needed the rest. As he dozed fitfully, he thought of the next day's errands—return the van and chainsaw, retrieve his car from the garage and make it appear to anyone, at the college and elsewhere, that all was well, giving no indication of the murder and evasion he felt so guilty about.

As dawn broke, Mack took the van to an outdoor carwash facility. Dropping quarters into the machine, he stepped inside the back, waving the wand around, hoping to rinse away whatever traces may have been left of the crime. No one saw him, best he knew, though it occurred to him that cleaning the inside of a vehicle this way would grab attention and be the sort of sight someone would likely notice and remember. He returned the van to the rental agency, finished the paperwork, and walked to retrieve his car. Was the rug cleaned enough? Not likely. He remembered the store near his apartment that rented out rug-cleaning equipment, Carpet Corpsman, he thought, and decided to use those services. He rented a red device, looked something like a vacuum cleaner, and bought some solvent. Inside his apartment, he fiddled with the machine, almost beyond his skills, but shampooed all the rugs, wiped down the chainsaw, and wrapped it up in a blanket for another trip.

He first stopped at the grocery store and rolled the carpet cleaner up to the counter, back to where he had been only about two hours earlier. "Didn't take long, eh?" the twenty-something woman at the grocery store spoke to him with a smile. Mackey had not thought anyone would notice.

"No, small place," he replied, and tried to smile in return.

At the hardware store, Mackey feared that the skinny, short-haired kid who had rented the chainsaw to him might make connections. As he sat in the parking lot, he spotted a young man with a thick mop of rusty red hair, collecting aluminum cans for recycling. Mackey approached him and spoke gently, and he hoped, in an innocuous tone.

"Sorry to bother you, son, but could you do me a favor? I'm in a terrible hurry and hurt my back a bit, so could you please take this chainsaw into the store for me?" He handed the young guy a fifty, which made his face light up.

"Sure—glad to."

Mackey took off in his car, nervously drumming his fingers on the steering wheel, and looking back at the store. He knew his next step—return to his office, try to relax with the techniques he had learned from yoga, and act like nothing had happened. Witnesses if they were called would say, "Oh, he was fine, his regular self." Just stroll around, look casual. Somewhere in the back of his mind, he kept wondering, *Was there anything I left at the college?*

16

MANUEL ZACHARIAS, WHOM everyone called Zach, dismounted from his tractor and began his daily routine of making sure everything was ready to roll by dawn. He was a good worker, enjoyed his job, and got along with almost everyone because of his gentle but strong persona, even though he spoke little English. Daylight was just breaking, and he gazed across the rugged landscape. Off to his left, he spotted something that made no sense—a mannequin? It must be one of those dummies his sons had practiced on in their martial arts class, a big white man with no arms, but who would toss away something like that, and why, especially out here, far from town?

Slowly walking up closer, he felt horror course through his body—a trunk and head, no limbs, looked like one of those rock stars from the punk bands his kids listened to. Hardly able to breathe, he began to yell out, saw only Larry, the barrel-chested gringo who supervised him, but spoke no Spanish, so he ran to Armando, his Costa Rican coworker who spoke both languages fluently, and spilled out his discovery in discordant gasps.

Armando had trouble understanding his friend and could only imagine that Zach was mistaken about what he had just seen in the rows, but called out to Larry to join them to find out what, for sure, had been dumped on the property. Larry and Armando both drew back in shock at what they saw, staggered, and tried to come to their senses.

Larry spoke out, urgency in his voice, "Call the sheriff—no, I will, and Armando, tell the boss. Zach, stay here, and answer any questions the deputies ask, okay?"

Armando translated, and Zach nodded his head, bowed slightly, said a silent prayer from his childhood, and waited for the authorities to appear. He knew it would be the longest day of his life, and it had barely begun.

The first uniforms on the scene had witnessed plenty of bloody crimes, but the blaring inhumanity of what looked back at them was past any of the shootings or wrecks of their careers. They quickly sealed off the area while a Spanish-speaking officer pumped Zach for any information, which was nothing more than the time and location of the discovery. Others snapped photos, called in to homicide, and made a tacit agreement that the big shots would be handling everything else.

By the time the detectives showed up, cameras were flashing and small bits of evidence—cigarette butts, hairs, trash—were all "bagged and tagged."

The body was later repositioned to capture the wounds and garish tattoos, which every cop recognized as the generic markings of white trash jailbirds. A crudely drawn outline of a snake, with "Water Moccasin" written below it (his street name?) and "White Knights." Best guess on the latter was that it was a gang he hooked up with, probably while doing time. The evenness of the cuts at the shoulders and hips led detectives to conjecture it was the work of a large motorized cutting mechanism, most likely a chainsaw. Noting all this information, the cops went to work—they would seek out every outlet that may have recently sold a chainsaw nearby and go nationwide about the youth's tattoos and see if fingerprints found at the scene could make a match.

Word had leaked out and every newspaper, small and large, had reporters and camera crews buzzing. The TV and radio stations had also dispatched their agents, and soon Phoenix was on fire with the word of a horrendous crime, the type that makes headlines. By the end of the day, Zach's unsettling discovery was on nationwide news.

The investigating officers had no way of knowing this, but their first line of inquiry was about to be answered, with little effort on their part, thanks to the exceptional stupidity of the perpetrator. Back in Phoenix, young Rhett sat down for another of his mundane chores, cleaning out the returned chainsaws, brushing away those troublesome wisps of wood and whatever else may appear. The moment he opened up this one, his gut felt kicked in and he grimaced—there was blood! Had someone cut himself badly while using this? That didn't add up, especially with the amount he saw. Worse, while gritting his teeth, he focused on small white chunks of something, and Rhett could not think of it being anything but pieces of bone.

"Bill? You come here, please, right away? It's important."

His manager looked irritated, like "can't you handle this yourself?" As Bill looked at what Rhett showed him, he froze in horror and spoke the words that would suddenly start to bring the pieces together.

"Call the cops."

An entire crew of police appeared quickly and gathered up and took the chainsaw to the lab. Two remained to ask questions of Rhett. He handed over the photo, rental invoice, credit card info, and tried to describe the bungler who had rented it.

"Oh, fifty-five or sixty, not too tall, sloppy, wearing a weird hat, and he spoke with a lisp or something. He was alone and acted nervous. Didn't see what he drove. Can't remember if he returned it or someone else did. I think it was the only time I saw him." Rhett looked upset, almost reluctant, as he spoke these words.

The cops thanked him, gave him a card, and encouraged him to call if he remembered anything else. After they left, Rhett asked to go home early, which Bill granted, and he sulked in his apartment all day, unable to rid his mind of the nightmare.

17

THE "NOT TOO tall, sloppy" professor had made it back to the college campus, unaware of the folly he had made, and strolled, trying to show an aura of "doesn't have a care in the world" in his gait. Mackey walked through the quad, surrounded by myrtle trees. He took deep breaths, exhaled slowly, and entered the offices of the history department. Ronnie, a long-time secretary, who pretty much ran everything, greeted him with the slight trace of New York accent she still carried. Mackey smiled, tried to laugh lightly, and engaged in small talk with her.

"Oh, not much. A little bored really, so I came back here to catch up on paperwork." Mackey tried to convey to her and others that all was normal; he was not nervous or worried, so he whistled (something he did not normally do) because he always thought that was the sign of someone who was carefree. He sat in the chair behind his desk, looked through some mail, and waited about half an hour. He then walked down the hall, extended a casual greeting to his coworker, Phil Lake, whom he had always viewed as an ally, though the two men were quite different.

As he walked back to his car, he waved to the gardeners trimming the bushes and settled down in the driver's seat. So Ronnie, Phil and the gardeners, if ever questioned, would say, "Oh, he was as cool as a cucumber—no way he could have just committed any crime and been on the run. He acted like everything was normal."

Mackey might not have been so confident had he known about the gruesome discovery and the police follow-up. With little haste, warrants had been issued to search his apartment, house, car and office. There was also a warrant for his arrest. If he had known that, he may not have made tracks back to his apartment but to his house, in hopes of destroying anything incriminating, although nothing there related at all to Travis. There was, however, literally pounds of videos showing his behavior with other youngsters, probably not identifiable or for sure underage, but strong enough to support what the prosecution would claim: he was engaging in sexual behavior with young street hustlers, which was exactly what Travis Kingman had been, for years, if he were found and identified.

It might have been a while before the police determined the identity of the trashed torso, but they knew that Francis DeSales Mackey, history professor at Arizona State, was either the killer, or at the very least an accomplice or accessory to the crime. Undercover agents were already tailing him, making notes of his travel and behavior and feeding information back to Robbery and Homicide.

Someone like Travis would have known that the two hefty and tough-looking men in cheap suits standing by his apartment door were cops at first sight, but not Francis Mackey. Even as they approached him with grim faces and reached for their badges, he thought nothing of their appearance.

"Professor Francis Mackey?"

"Yes, gentlemen, what could I do for you?"

With both badges out and a warrant held up high, the more senior partner said, "Just come with us. We need to handcuff you."

Mackey did not have the personality to object but acted surprised, hoping that his reaction would lend to the belief of his innocence.

"Oh, this must be a mistake—I can't think of anything I have done for which I might be arrested," he spoke in a soft voice.

The arresting officers said nothing but cuffed and placed him in the back of their car and drove the suspect—so unlike most of those they arrested—downtown for questioning.

Once the three of them made it to the administration building, they entered an austere room where Mackey was uncuffed and offered anything to drink. Just some water, he said. One officer read him his Miranda rights, followed by Mackey giving them a quick lecture of the landmark case to show off his historical knowledge, to which they only nodded in a dull manner, and informed him of the report about a chainsaw with blood inside the chambers. Would he like to explain?

"Well, I guess the truth is out now," Mackey began with a sigh. "I better level with you and tell you about the misconduct of my friend and me. More of an acquaintance, really. Troy Anson, young lad with rusty red hair. We were driving along, outside of town, past the biker hangout, the ones called the Mephistos, when there was a rough bump, a yelp, and we realized he had run over and killed one of their pit bulls. Those bikers are so violent and vindictive, and we knew they would stomp us to death with their big boots. We both panicked, could think of nothing to do but quickly bring the dead beast into his car and run. But Troy felt we had to cover tracks better, so he had me rent the chainsaw, and he cut the body up—I would have no idea how to operate such a thing, nor the stomach for it— placed the carcass in a black plastic bag, and said he would dispose of it, and return the saw. That was the last I saw of him. I guess not reporting killing a dog is a misdemeanor, and dumping the remains also, but that is all this is about."

Both experienced cops knew his story was a crock but asked for a description of the car where they might find Anson. Very subtly, Officer Number Two opened the next bag.

"You don't know anything of any other crimes, do you? Got any other boyfriends, younger, into the punk scene, maybe?"

Mackey gulped, shook his head in the negative, and asked if he were free to go. They instructed him about his right for bail, how it might take a while, but they would be in touch. Not just in touch, but watching him every minute, which a jerk like him would probably not even notice.

And as sure they were, the story they had just heard was a fabrication, they knew from years of work that they would have to follow up, look for holes in the story, before it could gain any credibility. They drove a few miles, past the outskirts of town, into a lonely looking and dusty area, out to Mephisto headquarters, which looked almost serene in midday, and found a familiar face, dressed in leather and denim, with a body as broad as both of them put together, and ragged hair down to his elbows. He called out to them.

"Button. McIntosh. What are you two doing out here? We ain't done nothin'."

"Didn't say you did, Heavy Duty. Need a little info. You wouldn't be missing any dogs around here, would you?

"Dogs?" The burly biker looked genuinely puzzled. When cops came, it was about drugs or missing chicks, but not dogs. He ran his thick fingers through his bushy beard and answered calmly, "No, we got five, all accounted for. If you want to question them, go ahead," and laughed at his own joke.

"So none missing. Pit bulls, are they?"

"No, man, we got Rottweilers, always have. There was a gang from Vegas hung out here a year or so back, they had pit bulls, but no, just our Rottweilers."

"Thanks, Heavy Duty—won't be back anytime soon."

"Sure hope not," he mumbled to himself as he watched them drive off.

18

THE ACCOUNT OF the grisly find was all over the television, but Bryce was not the type to follow the news too closely, so he sat in his favorite coffee shop, nursing a mocha, and eyeing the pastries. While he usually didn't say such things aloud, he would have sounded more like a woman—not surprisingly—with his thoughts of "Oh no, can't have that! Must think of my waistline!" It was while in his private thoughts that his eyes fell on an untidy pile of newspapers on the table in front of him, with the headline on the front page, about a torso discovered, and the arrest of a history professor. Like anyone else, he was intrigued, also stunned by the article, but the description of the victim made Bryce jump.

"Young, white male, muscular, tattoos, Mohawk-style hair . . . " With all of his heart, he wished the remains were not those of his casual friend, but the possibility alone drove him to the nearest pay phone, where he called the number in the article asking for anyone with any information to notify police. After being on hold about ten minutes, and listening to dentist-office music, Bryce finally got a human voice. He spilled out everything, describing the tattoos and how Travis—that's what he said his name was, did not tell him his last name—talked about extortion.

"Oh, here's a tip. He said he was from Owensboro, Kentucky. That should narrow it down. Sure—I'll come downtown to tell you all I know."

The investigators decided to jump on Bryce's one piece of information and called authorities in Owensboro. After being filled in with a description, specifically the tattoo "Water Moccasin," officers there in the juvenile department felt confident they knew who it was—Travis Kingman, seventeen, small time but repeat offender. After exchanging contact numbers, the Owensboro team assured Phoenix that they would send out all they had, and suggested towns across the river in Indiana get a call—this kid got in trouble everywhere.

Bryce was not the only one to think he may know something about the case. Back from Gateway, on a long run, Gavin McKeevy was relaxing in his hotel room, catching up on the news he had missed while supervising loads. Featured prominently was the story about the dismembered youth and how the police had a lead but were not saying anything concrete yet. His mind moved back to what he had seen a few nights ago and wondered, with ample doubt, if he had seen anything connected to the crime. There was a picture of Mackey, but McKeevy had not seen enough of a face in dark night to say for sure if the figure in the shadows and on the screen were one and the same but looked close enough.

As if he had taken a cue from Bryce, McKeevy got on line and waited nervously for someone to talk to. Eventually, he got an ear to listen to him, and he described the scene, where it was, and a vague description. "Fifties or sixties, about my height, five-nine, and wearing what looked like wire rim glasses. And a pullover hat with no brim, or maybe it was a wig. Oh, another thing—there was a rental truck that said, 'Homan Haulers.'"

After asking him to wait while conferring with superiors, the female voice left for a minute, came back and told him, "Mr. McKeevy, we are sending a car out to take you to the on-ramp you described. Wait there and officers will arrive soon."

Indeed they did, with others in tow in different cars, and McKeevy gave the directions with the ease of an experienced trucker. At the on-ramp, he pointed to the exact spot where he had seen someone, and officers busied themselves with yellow tape, and others approached with evidence-gathering tools. A stench told the officers they were on to something, and within an hour, the extremities of Travis Kingman were gathered, photographed and bagged.

Another group of detectives was assigned to Homan Haulers with a warrant. If they had a record of Mackey renting the van as described by McKeevy, whose word would be valuable since he knew his trucks, it would be one more strand that they could weave into a noose. Without a doubt, the case was on its way.

19

Brodie

SITTING IN HIS comfortable office, detective Nelson Brodie, who went by Nick, was telling an old story to some of the cadets, those young enough not to have heard it already. His voice, gravelly by nature, drawled somewhat, but gave off an affable tone, with animation and vivid gestures.

"So we were playing this Quaker team from Nebraska, right? I was defense. One of them said I was playing too rough, confronted me, and I just waved him off. He pointed and said, 'Then I must teach *thee* better.' Yeah, he actually said *thee*. We line up at scrimmage, and I break through, I see the big guy with his eyes way down the field, and I think, 'Ha! He doesn't even see me coming. I'm gonna sack the quarterback, they'll lose ten yards—this game is mine!' Then I see this white blur, hear a crack, and wonder—'Hey, who turned out the lights?'—I crawled off to the sidelines on my hands and knees, blood all over my jersey. Yep, he taught me better. How I got this nose."

He always rubbed his crooked nose when he got to that point of the story. The cadets laughed and gave him the attention he so craved.

Some coworkers wondered if Brodie ever did much of anything. Most knew the truth—he had what seemed like idle time, but when some hardcore, old-fashioned digging had to be done and done right, Brodie was that kind of cop, and one who never gave up.

When his audience left, he picked up the phone and pressed a button to the floor below him.

"Montijo? Brodie. Got one for ya. There are three guys standing on the edge of a roof. One white, one black, one Mexican. They all fall off at the same time. Which one will hit the sidewalk last? Give up? The Mexican will stop to write some graffiti on the way down." He chuckled with his pal, and began looking through a pile of junk mail the whole department had accumulated.

At this point, two plainclothesmen, followed by a secretary in uniform, rushed in, laughing absurdly, with one of the few female employees following behind, shaking her head in disbelief.

"Brodie! Latest technique from headquarters! You know how to give a wetback CPR? Can't touch a wetback's lips, right? So it's like this . . ."

They both cupped their hands around their mouths, looking like they were about to shout something to a distance, raised their feet up and pretended to stomp on the suspect's chest, while breathing out heavily from feet above where the invisible criminal lay.

"You guys are crazy," the secretary told them, but laughed along with them. All three ventured out with Brodie watching them, leaning back and with a look about him that gave off a sense of not boredom or tedium, but the quiet look of someone trapped inside an office, not out on patrol, because he had gotten old, by cop standards—forty-seven.

That tedium ended soon enough, with the arrival of Tom Goddard, an obnoxious redhead that was often abrasive, and sometimes used excessive force when subduing unruly suspects. Brodie knew who was entering his office before he looked up, hearing this faked Southern accent calling out in a singsong voice.

"*Sur-prise, sur-prise, sur-prise!*" Carrying a considerable bundle of folders in his hands and an annoying smile on his face, he plunked the pile on the desk of the older and more experienced detective, smugly.

"You never guessed who would head up the investigation on that kid who got cut to pieces and dumped by some psycho. So here it all is, and you will be one busy Okie for a while." He left, still chuckling to himself.

No, Brodie was not surprised. He figured from the start the top brass would lean on him, with his diligence, to handle this case. It reminded him so much of a homicide from his childhood he had heard about. Was it Long Beach? A girl had been cut in half and her body dumped at the foot of one the oil rigs the town was known for. He could not think of her name, but it haunted him, how demeaning the murder, and the horror her family and friends must have felt.

Brodie sat quietly for a moment, looking at his desktop littered with paper clips, notes, unopened mail, and some licorice he had bought for his kids, now living in the suburbs with their mom and new stepdad. Yes, he was an Okie, one of those who stopped short of California after his family escaped the Dust Bowl, and carried with him a strong sense of justice. Nobody, no matter how poor or how far fallen, deserved to have their lives cut short and tossed away like that girl in Long Beach or this poor Kentucky kid. Brodie sat silently, his chin in his hands, and thought deeply, not so much about the particulars of the case but its moral impact.

He knew two things for sure.

A monster had done this.

And a monster was going to pay.

20

I N THE CONFERENCE room, Nick Brodie stood at the head of a table, with half a dozen subordinate officers seated around him, each with a copy of the information so far gathered about the Mackey-Kingman case. They all wore polyester suits, with white dress shirts and ties, but the ties were always askew, partly undone, or somehow unkempt enough to let any observer know these were cops, not businessmen. Some smoked, some chewed gum, and all had an expression that mixed anxiety with a trace of boredom. Brodie addressed them in a laconic voice.

"Gentlemen—using the term loosely—this is what we got. Let's start with the vic. Seventeen going on forty with a rap sheet going back a few years. Police in his hometown busted him for drug offenses, shoplifting, and some misdemeanors. Did time, beat the shit out of two other inmates at once, reasons unknown, and had time added for that. Apparently belonged to a white supremacist gang called the 'White Knights,' local outfit. He even had a beef with the Feds."

"The Feds?" six voices all rang out in unison, and with a tone of incredulity as if they had just been told the leader of the PLO had converted to Judaism.

"Yep," Brodie continued. "Seems our guy was in middle school when Reagan was shot that time. History teacher said, let's all be nic-ey-nicey and send the President good wishes. Didn't check the letters before mailing them to the White House, so a week later who comes to the school? One of our friends from the Secret Service. Travis had both insulted and, in a sense, threatened Reagan. Agent gave him a good talking to, let him off with a warning, and told him the record would be kept, so here it is—sent me a copy of the letter as well."

The other officers looked at Brodie and gestured as if to say, "Come on, let's hear it."

Never one to miss an opportunity for showmanship, Brodie cleared his throat, assumed a cordial tone, and recited the contents:

Dear Ronnie—you are doing a shitty job.
You asshole, you should legalize pot and cocaine.
I'm glad you got shot, you stupid, jack-off, son of a bitch.

After some chuckles and guffaws, Brodie informed them further, "Real bright kid—misspelled 'legalize,' 'cocaine,' and even 'bitch'—left out the *t*. Not an honor student by any means."

"Hey!" one of the team interjected. "He should have signed it, 'Jimmy Carter.'"

That set the laughter rolling again, with heads shaking in disbelief. A bizarre crime, tragic with humorous moments, tragicomic in the worst sense.

After the laughing quieted down, Brodie went on. "Then the perp—no priors, hardly any traffic offenses, but word on the street is he was real deviant, into taking pictures of young guys, may or may not have been of age. Clearly nonviolent until now, even passive, and his coworkers all say he hated guns and avoided conflict."

The other officers listened attentively, with enough experience among them to know such crimes have been committed by otherwise law-abiding types. They all knew the defense would present this at trial—that how and why, all of a sudden, would a calm, educated man kill someone and dismember his remains? How would two such different types cross paths, let alone set up a relationship?

Brodie interrupted their thoughts. "Status of the evidence—no weapon found, but blood in his apartment, the moving van, and most significantly, the chainsaw with blood and bone, his picture from the store, a witness there, plus a trucker that saw him at the on-ramp where the limbs were found."

"Is this guy an idiot or what?" interrupted one of the detectives, with his associates nodding in agreement.

"He could have just bought the chainsaw then ditched it, like he did the gun," Goddard added.

"Yeah, or, since he did rent it, toss it, then say he lost it and would pay for it. We may not have caught him, otherwise," another noted. Every cop in the room was thinking the same thing—a real dumb son of a bitch.

Brodie continued, "Another witness, so to speak, is a casual friend of the vic. Name's Bryce Whorley, a fruitcake who had a number of conversations with him. He's willing to testify that Travis was planning on blackmailing one of his clients and that could establish a motive. To avoid blackmail, Mackey killed the poor kid and trashed his body, thinking no one would ever miss him."

"Cops search his house, nice place in a respectable suburb, lawn covered with cement, pretty barren inside. Found cartons of homemade videos, all of young guys jacking off, stuff like that. In one room, looks like he was covering the walls with soundproofing materials."

All the cops muttered in disgust, thinking of what had gone on in Mackey's sick head.

"He cleaned out his apartment, but they found a couple photos hidden away. Also, there was a whole package of pictures of Kingman from the vic's hotel room, including one of him and Mackey looking real buddy-buddy." Brodie paused for any comments.

"Bet that's what the kid kept in an effort to blackmail Mackey," another officer conjectured.

"Yeah, I thought that, too, but no way to prove it," Brodie asserted. "Also, a surveillance video from a store near Mackey's apartment, showing the two of them on a brief shopping errand."

After some more discussion, Brodie began to summarize.

"So the case is pretty firm. The defense will claim no eyewitnesses, just ear, his downstairs neighbor, no weapon, and no apparent motive. Once the lab confirms that the remnants are human, we catch him in a lie, and will be on more solid ground. If we could find that gun or something connecting him to it, then we could hammer away at him, but for now, this is what we got."

Nick Brodie had no way of knowing this, but such a development was in the works. In the quiet history department office back at the college, Ronnie the secretary was cleaning out old files, stacking up the term papers that she had seen too many of over the decades, when something shiny, with a sheet of paper, caught her eye. It looked like a rod, and two tiny plastic bottles of liquids, in a case that might have held a pen and pencil set. The paper was a receipt, with the name of a gun retailer at the top, so she took pause. Ronnie knew enough from all the crime shows she watched on TV not to touch anything, but quickly called the police to report her find, and waited quietly for officers to appear. She told them everything in her professional manner, and the officers gathered the evidence, wrote down a statement, thanked her, and returned to headquarters.

The next morning, Brodie and his team felt almost elated. Now was the time to call in the killer and let him squirm, catch him in his contradictions, and set a trap for him. With a lot of luck, the bungling perpetrator would hang his head, confess to what he had done, and save the taxpayers a bundle. Or this could be a real dogfight, if Mackey got himself lawyered up with just the right combination of sleazeballs to defend him. That was too often the case, as any cop knew.

By noon, the professor was admitted into the interrogation room and guided to a chair. Mackey tried to sit back a bit, as he would have to lord over one of his students, but he found that impossible. In fact, the chair was bolted and had a slight tilt forward. The positioning was uncomfortable and made him feel vulnerable, and hard to conceal his feelings, which was the exact intent of the setup. After mounting the recording equipment and reading the Miranda rights again, they asked if Mackey wanted a lawyer (no).

Brodie waded in, sounding almost folksy.

"So, Dr. Mackey, let's look at the facts. Lab results are in, confirming that the blood and bone found in the chainsaw were human and the same type as the victim. We have a witness that you rented the chainsaw, and another who says he saw you at the off-ramp carrying something out to the ivy. And we could not find a gun, but a cleaning kit was found in your office with a partial print, matching one of your fingers, on the rod." Brodie glared at the nervous little man as he spoke in a deadpan, and two deputies joined in the grilling, knowing someone who was not a career criminal would crash soon.

Mackey lowered his head, rubbed his hands over his face, and breathed audibly. After a long pause, he began to speak in a soft voice, trying not to look up at the three men who were confronting him.

"All right, the time has come for the truth." Again, he paused, waited a few moments before recanting. Every cop knows—the longer it takes for someone to answer, the more likely what follows is a lie.

"On that night, I was in my apartment with Travis, a fellow I knew somewhat and had a causal relationship with. He was always milking me for money, and I gave him some now and then, and never asked for any of it back. He was something of a leech, but not enough to drain my finances. Also, there was Troy Anson, in his twenties, and more acquainted with Travis. The discussion became heated between the two of them, something about money Travis owed, and I tried to cool things down, as I always do. Some insults flew back and forth, so I offered to go into the kitchen and whip up ice cream treats. From the kitchen, I could hear the voices rising and the argument intensifying, so I returned to the living room, and saw that Troy had found the handgun I kept near my reading chair, ever since I had been threatened by some bullies, and was pointing it at Travis. Troy was shaking violently, and the gun went off, perhaps accidentally, but then Troy put another bullet into the back of his head, as I stood there, petrified. I thought he might have shot me as well, so when he ordered me to move the body and fetch some kitty litter, and later to rent a van and chainsaw. I obeyed."

Brodie and his partners watched Mackey closely all the time, his eyes repeatedly shifting to his left, a clear sign of deception. They also listened to the pauses as he progressed, indicating that he was making up information as he moved along.

"By the next day, I had provided all the materials, and Anson carved up the body. I could not watch that, of course. He told me to dispose of the limbs while he would ditch the torso and the gun. I cleaned out the van while he worked on the apartment. He scared me some more and said he was fleeing to Mexico. I know, I should have called the police, but he may have killed me, or I might have been implicated in the homicide, and I just panicked. I realize I made some terrible mistakes, but I am not the killer. Troy Anson was, and I hope he gets caught."

Len Button, second in command, addressed the professor in a bland tone. "Dr. Mackey, would you be willing to take a lie detector test?"

Mackey bolted up, or tried to, and began a lecture. "Polygraph results are inadmissible in court, as courts have ruled at both state and federal levels for years. You are wasting your time," he stated, sounding highly self-confident.

The professor was educated and erudite enough to know court rulings and their impact, even citing the cases, but not cagey enough to know the real reason why police ask that question—to see how the accused reacts, and enable them to know what the defendant was thinking.

Now they knew.

All three of the detectives knew that Troy Anson was a variation of "my naughty twin did it," but kept calm. Brodie informed the lisping suspect that he was under arrest for the murder of Travis Kingman, and the district attorney would be filing charges soon. Bail would be set, and now was the time to look for a lawyer.

21

Bantley.

T HE OFFICE OF Bantley and Corcoran stood prominently along the busy streets of downtown Phoenix. Both lawyers had appeared in the news frequently, flamboyant and expensive, although willing to take a case for a lower fee if the publicity would feed their egos and insure future clients. Each had a reputation for being an unethical lawyer (most cops would say that was a redundant phrase) and defended clients they knew, from the start, to be patently guilty.

Grant Bantley sat at his spacious desk, fingering a pile of extra-strength breath mints. They were so powerful, he could not stand them, but needed them to cover the smell of liquor on his breath, even at midday. His buttoned vest fit a bit too snugly across his thick middle, once solid muscle now beginning to flag, and he flexed his arms, summoning up the inner strength he still held, a former college boxer, tough and determined, formidable in the courtroom. His New England accent stood out in the West, a blue blood from the wealthy avenues of Newport, Rhode Island, and his career had soared. Once he heard people say about the Mackey case, "No one can get this moron off," he thought, *Oh, yes, someone can,* and smirked. He knew this case would put him in the spotlight, and he we was up for the challenge.

He sized up his opposition. The prosecutor was a likable, owlish sort who would cling to the facts (a topic Bantley would avoid, since facts usually indicated guilt) and present a logical argument that the police had, indeed, apprehended the true culprit, who had contradicted himself repeatedly and had acted as guilty as hell. That would be no match for Bantley's theatrics, playing on the emotions of the jury and the public, inflaming them with issues that had nothing to do with the case, but swaying them away from a guilty verdict. Plus, stir up some doubt.

The judge was an affable man. Louis Sandlin, a light-skinned African-American who would counsel the jury thoughtfully, rule prudently, but Bantley knew he could get away with some antics in the courtroom because Judge Sandlin always wanted to come across as a nice guy. The judge was never his first concern.

His first concern was the jury. He knew the secret: to get the right verdict, get the right jury. Find at least a few who are scared of the system, resentful of the law, and they would play into his hands. Doing this for a white, Anglo defendant would not be easy, and not too many people would sympathize with a known homosexual, and perhaps a predatory one. Attack the victim, fight dirty, and hope to make at least one juror waver.

He himself had been on trial once for drunken driving. His attorney had gotten him off by ranting against the police, their racism and bigotry. Even though Bantley was as white as a marshmallow, and his English ancestry went back to colonial times, he had been acquitted. Of course he was guilty, he had never imagined otherwise, but he knew what cards to play.

He had met with his client and coached him on the basics—what to wear, how to carry himself and what tone of voice to assume. What the professor had to do was to project the right image: this is a passive, nonviolent gentle type who never has nor ever would commit such an act of violence. Also—and this was the easy part—show them that the sixty-year old bungler was not competent enough, not crafty enough, to have engineered this. Bantley had to stifle a laugh whenever he read about how brainlessly Mackey had done the deed and attempted to cover his tracks.

When Bantley met with Prof. Mackey, he did not waste time asking about guilt or innocence, just to make sure to plead not guilty, look the part, and let the lawyer do most of the talking. Appearance was a priority—have Mackey shave, wear conservative suits and ties, and look vulnerable, even weak. Make those jurors think you are just not the type, and they will follow that lead, no matter where the evidence points. He also coached the professor on proper tone of voice and posturing, because he was for sure going to testify on his own behalf. Sometimes keeping your mouth shut worked best, but Bantley knew the jury would be swayed by listening to the weak voice and seeing a man incapable, both physically and mentally, of having carried out this crime.

And then there was the voir dire. He knew his opposition, the assistant district attorney, would weed through them, looking for conventional types who would not give an inch to someone they knew was guilty. Neither the victim nor the accused were model citizens, but the prosecution would point out the brutality of the crime, especially the desecration that followed. He, Bantley, would winnow out any religious types, or rednecks, who would be biased against his client because of his sexual orientation. Look for social liberals, and people who mistrusted the police—he knew how to find those.

As expected, the judge, the Honorable Louis Sandlin, combed through the prospective jurors, introduced them to both the defense and prosecution, and began the selection process. After describing the case and the state's claim, the judge allowed both attorneys to interview the twenty-some men and women of various ages, occupations and ethnicities. His opponent, a scholarly and well-spoken gentleman, stressed how strong the evidence was and for everyone to concentrate on the facts and testimony, not to be swayed by emotions. Bantley kept it general, talking about reasonable doubt, and took a fairly mild tone (by his standards) to deliver the message that it was their job to find his client not guilty—he would save the heavy artillery for later. It took the better part of the day, but twelve jurors and two alternates remained, more men than women, with some nonwhites, two Latinos and a Filipino, and Bantley faintly smiled.

He pondered his opening statements. He knew his opponent would be assertive, stating that the physical evidence was mountainous, the accused's account was not just a fabrication, but a ridiculous one at that, how eyewitnesses placed him at the scene of at least part of the body disposal, and his contradictions as the case progressed—in short, slam dunk, the state wins.

But Bantley was the drama king. He would come on with passion, stressing how his client had been railroaded by the police, who had the wrong man and knew it, but needed a fall guy so they could claim victory, and look at the humble professor—does he look or act like a killer? No way. The DA wants to catch a big fish, and this is his chance, but do not let this injustice prevail! Yes—he could win this case.

22

The trial.

THE COURTROOM LOOKED like any other in the country, just more packed than usual, with the media in attendance. When the arrival of Judge Sandlin was announced, all stood respectfully and waited for the slightly pudgy black man to take his seat and look about thoughtfully. His honor spoke to the jury, offered some instructions, and indicated for the prosecution to make an opening statement.

The Assistant District Attorney, Joel Penn, was distinguished, younger than expected, but gave off an air of confidence and professionalism. He drove home to the jury what the accused had done, never faltered in his conviction, and explained how the state would call witnesses who saw Mackey and Travis together, had seen Mackey disposing of body parts, that Mackey had changed his story and contradicted himself, and the motive—either rage or an effort to quell an extortion scheme. Every juror listened to him and tried not to show any leanings, but the contentions made were compelling.

When Grant Bantley approached the jury, a hush fell and every eye riveted on him. There was something about how he carried himself so confidently, and his baritone voice echoed with strength.

"This is nothing new. The police grabbed someone they knew they could convict, not because of evidence, but that they knew many would jump to the conclusion of his guilt due to his secret life, the prejudice against homosexuals, and the emotional nature of this case. They have no weapon, no witness to the murder, and no viable motive, so they have put Professor Mackey, a man with absolutely no criminal record in his sixty years, not even a misdemeanor, a man known to be passive and submissive, and have offered him up as a sacrifice while the real culprit remains at large, to cover up their failure. The defense will show that not only did the professor not commit this crime, he is incapable of it. His fate, and the fate of anyone falsely accused, lies in your hands."

All were silent, almost breathless, when the judge announced that the prosecution could call its first witness.

"The state calls Manuel Zacharias."

Zach approached the witness chair, accompanied by an interpreter, and was sworn in. Morgan asked about the discovery of the body, time and location. The answers flowed in, calmly describing the gruesome morning, and his coworkers also verified his story. Bantley declined to cross-examine anyone until after one of the detectives from the scene of the discovery spoke.

"From your records, detective, did anyone see who deposited the torso at the ranch?" Bantley asked, veiled accusation in the tone.

"No, no one," the detective replied, mildly.

"Any physical evidence gathered at the scene to lend a clue?"

"A few cigarette butts, nothing else."

"That is all, thank you."

Penn spoke briefly of the paper record and photo of Mackey at the hardware store and called another witness. Once Rhett was sworn in and seated, the district attorney gently led him though the moments at the store. Yes, that was definitely him, pointing to Mackey and describing him.

When asked if anything seemed unusual, Rhett proffered, "Besides being super nervous, he seemed like a real spazz, someone who could not handle the chainsaw. I had my reservations about renting it to him. But I did, took his picture, and he left, alone. When the chainsaw was returned, I cleaned it, and found blood inside, so we called the police."

"Thank you. Your witness," Penn wrapped up, gesturing to Bantley.

"Mr. Quincy, did you see the accused after this incident?" he asked.

"Not that I recall."

"But the chainsaw was returned, undeniably, and if neither you nor your coworkers saw Professor Mackey, it was likely someone else who returned it."

"Could be. I don't remember who brought it back. Some customers just drop it off without the paperwork."

"No more questions."

More witnesses followed: lab technicians who verified that the blood inside the chainsaw was human and that of Travis, also found in the rental van, and the defense sat back impassively. No, there were no questions, no one denied that the chainsaw and van were used for disposing of the body. Same routine for the blood traces, minute, found on the carpet and around the bathroom. Again, there was no debate about the locale of the killing, just who had administered it.

The next two witnesses, however, did come under Bantley's scrutiny. For the employee at Homan Haulers, he pressed on. "Was anyone else in the van? The professor may have rented it, but someone else could have driven it, right?" And to the long-haired, gorgeous guy who worked at the gun store, his recollection of Mackey was sure, but Bantley pushed another topic.

"You say he looked inexperienced? Like he had no idea what to do with that gun? He needed advice on how to load it? Is that how most of your customers are? Mackey was not the type to own a gun, let alone use one, so might this suggest he bought the gun on someone else's behest?" Bantley pursued.

The last question was objected to, speculative, and Judge Sandlin ordered the jury to ignore it, but Bantley knew he had just planted another seed of doubt. Just keep planting more, play on emotions, and the jury was his.

The state's next witness walked to the front of the courtroom, was sworn in, and assumed her seat with an air of dignity and composure. Every workplace had someone like Ronnie Hasson, just a secretary, but the one who knew where everything was, how to find anything, every channel for every procedure and the paperwork that followed. Speaking with hints of her New York origins, calmly and clearly, she described how she found the receipt and cleaning kit, which had Mackey's fingerprint on it, and how it had been secreted behind old term papers. Yes, she immediately contacted the police, and yes, she was careful not to disturb anything around the discovery site. Bantley passed on cross examination, knowing that Mackey had admitted he had bought the gun for his protection, but felt unsettled about the date of the purchase—two days before the shooting—that would be hard to pass off as a coincidence.

Witnesses from the university appeared, who attested to Mackey's calm demeanor when they saw him shortly after the killing—looked untroubled, same as usual, nothing suspicious. Many, including Professor Phil Lake, one of his closest associates, expanded on how Mackey was often the peacemaker at meetings, one who avoided conflict, and sometimes called "Mack the Mollifier." As Lake stepped down from the witness stand, Mackey softly whispered "Thank you" to his former associate.

From the comfort of his easy chair, Ed Cudahy read the accounts in his newspaper with disgust. He rolled his head from side to side, thinking of how abrasive and offensive the pathetic little man had been to him. He read further the words of Damian Mackey, the younger brother priest who helped the downtrodden of New Haven. He had always looked up to his big brother, who had no violent tendencies and hated guns. Ed had heard Mackey preach against the Second Amendment repeatedly, but also knew what a hypocrite his old professor had been and still remained.

The last of the article stated how testimony would resume the next Monday. He set the newspaper down, turned off the nearby lamp, and rested his eyes. Sleep would not come easily tonight, thinking about his past encounters with Mackey, and wondered what other lives he may have impacted, students and poor souls like that Kingman kid and all the young men who appeared in the photos found at Mackey's house. Think of the clerk who made the bloody find, that trucker who witnessed the dumping, and whatever friends the victim had. Yes, next week's testimony would be more agonizing, and the defense would pull out every dirty trick imaginable.

23

THE NEXT MONDAY, Judge Sandlin resumed the case, allowing the prosecution to call its next witness. Gavin McKeevy had dressed up a might for his appearance, looking more like a businessman than the trucker he was. In a deep, smooth voice, he described how he had stopped off that night (yes, to relieve himself, a bit embarrassed) and sighting the van with the sign that read "Homan Haulers," and the shadow of a man fitting Mackey's description.

When allowed to cross-examine the trucker, Bantley casually approached the stand, assuming a stance that was almost passive. Mackey had admitted to disposing of the limbs, so there was no need to hammer too hard.

"Mr. McKeevy, how would you describe the behavior of the individual in the ivy that night?"

"He looked very nervous, scared even, looking around all the time."

"Any idea why he might have been so scared?"

"Objection—speculative," Joel Penn's voice interrupted.

"Sustained."

"Did he seem to be alone to you?" Bantley asked this question with little passion.

"I saw no one else," McKeevy replied.

"No further questions."

Bryce Whorley next testified. He had performed before huge crowds, acting and dancing since his teens; so appearing in front of an audience was a cinch for him, but he displayed some nervousness sitting down and leaning toward the mike. The DA, Joel Penn, approached Bryce and spoke in a friendly manner.

"Bryce Whorley, you knew the victim, Travis Kingman. Could you tell the jury about Travis and the days shortly before his death?" Penn was making the victim more human to the jurors, calling him by his first name and evoking sympathy.

"Well, I made his acquaintance downtown a few weeks ago."

"Mr. Whorley?" Judge Sandlin interrupted. "Can you please speak up? We can barely hear you."

Bryce took in extra breath and projected, a technique learned from drama class to make himself more audible. This was not the first time anyone had commented on how soft-spoken he was. All eyes were on the lithe witness, still boyish looking at thirty with his freckles and dimples.

Bryce continued his narrative, describing how he had met Travis, looking a bit embarrassed at admitting his lingering at a known hangout, telling, in abbreviated form, how Travis had stood up for him in the face of an aggressor, and how he had advised Travis to look for better customers. He showed signs of guilt at this point, realizing how his advice had led Kingman to Mackey and eventual death. The last comments, drawn out carefully by Penn, were how Travis had told Bryce that he was planning on blackmailing one of his clients, and in spite of Bryce's pleading, Travis seemed determined to go through with his intent. As always, Penn gracefully nodded to the witness and made room for Bantley.

Bantley stood up, a big man, seeming bigger, slowly moving with the tough and confident swagger he had used when entering the ring, intimidating even before he spoke, and when his voice did ring out, the raw strength in its tone was enough to make a witness cower, which for someone as mild-mannered as Bryce Whorley, came across as terrifying. The questions fired away.

"You did not call the police when he told you his plans?" Bantley asked.

"No. Perhaps I should have, looking back."

"You say he was planning on blackmailing one of his clients, a doctor, right?" Bantley hammered on.

"Yes, he very specifically told me that."

"Mr. Whorley, have you ever told someone you were going to do something, and then ended up not going through with it?"

"Well, of course," Bryce stammered.

"So if Travis Kingman told you that, he may have just been dreaming, or trying to show off, or impress others, just maybe?"

"He sounded serious."

"Probably did—pretty serious-looking sort, wouldn't you say?"

"Oh, oh . . . he sounded serious," Bryce repeated.

"You also said, and I think this was your word, you *implored* him not to blackmail his client?" Bantley raised his voice slightly, sounding critical.

"That's right, I implored him."

"You sound like a persuasive type. Travis might have listened to you and not have gone through with his plan, do you agree?"

"Oh, he sounded like I did not convince him."

"And he said the target was a doctor, is that correct?"

"That is definitely correct. I remember clearly," Bryce said, trying to regain his self-confidence.

"Good. And you know that Professor Mackey is not a doctor, but a college professor, as does everyone else here."

"I do now, but . . . "

Bantley cut him off. "So if Travis Kingman *was* considering blackmailing anyone, it was a doctor, and not a teacher, and that would have nothing to do with Professor Mackey."

"Yes, but a professor is often called a doctor . . ."

"That is just blind guess work, Mr. Whorley!" Bantley interrupted.

"Objection. Badgering the witness," Joel Penn spoke up.

"Sustained." The judge leaned slightly forward. "Mr. Bantley, use a tone and approach less accusative."

"Yes, your honor," Bantley replied, feigning some compassion. But his plan had worked. One of the witnesses was reduced to shambles, and more doubt had been sown for the jury. Bantley also knew that jurors always wanted to know the *why* of any crime, not just the *how*. He thanked Bryce in what sounded like a considerate way and returned to his station, an aura of smugness surrounding him. Bryce stepped off from the witness stand, his head hanging down.

The rest of the afternoon was spent listening to detectives who had searched Mackey's apartment and house, some who had searched Travis's hotel room, and interviewed acquaintances of both the victim and the defendant. Bantley eased up on all of them, saving his invective for the leader of the investigation, the one who, if destabilized, could cause the state's case to weaken, and if he could play on the emotions of the jurors, pull off at least a hung jury.

Yes, Bantley was savoring his chance to pounce on the veteran, Nick Brodie, a showdown between two hardened men, one pursuing justice in the form of putting away a murderer, the other his own brand of justice, which embodied a way of thinking that whoever wins has achieved the right, even if a guilty party walks while the family of the victim grieves. One, a combat marine who had held firm in Korea against the toughest odds; the other, a former boxer, who lived for confrontations, the clash of two uncompromising forces.

When Judge Sandlin rapped his gavel at the end of that long afternoon, everyone in the courtroom, along with every member of the media, knew that the next day would be bumpy flight, so buckle down.

24

P ROCEDURES THE NEXT day seemed mundane at the outset, with the flow of detectives who explained the status of the evidence, how every piece led them to the professor, and the interviews, including Mackey's stumbling account of how he claimed the shooting of Travis had occurred. The later witnesses stressed how they felt Troy Anson, whom Mackey claimed killed Travis, was a product of Mackey's imagination, often used by criminals to refocus guilt onto a nonexistent party.

By noon, the judge called for a break. Some caught a quick lunch on the top floor, others idled around and chatted, but all seemed anxious. Everyone knew that a showdown was shaping up, like the anticipation of a match between two top athletes, the event all had been awaiting.

When the break was over, the courtroom refilled, with a buzz in the air, an atmosphere of excitement and dread somehow mixed together. All eyes were on the rugged man, so obviously a cop, with his craggy face and hardened demeanor. That included the eyes of Grant Bantley, who seemed to be saying, "Just wait, Mr. Tough Guy Detective."

Brodie was sworn in, and the prosecutor led him through a series of clear questions, with succinct answers following. Yes, the accused was advised of his rights, interrogated, gave two different and conflicting accounts of the night of the murder, both disproved, and Mackey admitted to being at least an accessory to the murder, cleaning the crime scene, procuring a moving van and chainsaw, and disposing of the limbs, and at no point was he observed with anyone else—he had acted alone. Brodie's delivery proved clear, assertive, and thorough. Joel Penn was too refined to make a "slam dunk" gesture, but he may as well have—the jurors all looked completely convinced.

This was the moment Grant Bantley had been relishing—the setting he knew he was born for, groomed for. He rose up to his full height, almost swaggered to the bench, and greeted the detective, who nodded back nonchalantly.

After a few cursory questions, Bantley pressed on.

"Detective Brodie, how diligently have you and your men searched for Troy Anson?"

"We questioned known associates of Kingman and Mackey, nearby residents of both parties, and no one had ever heard of him, or anyone fitting the description Mackey gave us," Brodie replied, with confidence, though he knew where the defense was leading him. Brodie added, "We even followed up on his"—Brodie paused, wanting to avoid an obscenity—"nonsense story about how he ran over a biker's dog."

Bantley pushed on. "Did you find anyone with the name Troy Anson?"

Brodie answered, "We did, but quickly eliminated him as being the individual described by the defendant."

"This Troy Anson did not fit the details provided by my client?" Bantley asked, sounding smug.

"Nowhere near it. He attends second grade in Fresno." Brodie's response was met with some light laughter in the courtroom.

Bantley continued, "Did you search for Anson the same way you go after other suspects, or were you dismissive, quick to assume my defendant was lying because you jumped to the conclusion of his guilt?"

"The notes of the interviews were recorded and a matter of record. We can produce them at any time." Brodie came back at the big man, with a tone and a glare that said, "I'm a Marine—I don't retreat in battle."

"Given your department's history of harassment and mistreatment of homosexuals, can we believe in the validity of the evidence gathered in this case? You and your officers want to make sure *someone* gets convicted and punished for this crime, is that about right?" Bantley nearly snarled.

Brodie waited a few seconds, thinking to himself, *Golden Gloves or not, I'd like to take this outside.* He maintained his cool and answered the question.

"If you're implying that any evidence was falsified or planted, you're wrong, and can't prove it because it never happened. In fact, Francis Mackey has never denied that it was his gun, his rental van, his rented chainsaw, and the blood in the apartment and inside the chainsaw were that of Travis Kingman, whose body was at least fifty miles away. So no, nothing was falsified in any way." Brodie let out a deep breath and tried to stay calm.

At this point, Bantley decided to toss out his last trick card, like a jack-in-the-box popping out unexpectedly.

"Detective Brodie, is it true that you and your cohorts exchange overtly racist jokes about Hispanics in your office?"

"Objection! Irrelevant and inflammatory!" Penn's voice yelled out.

"Sustained," said the judge in the flat speech that judges are famous for.

Bantley paused, moved about slightly, hoping that the last barb reached the few nonwhite jurors, and that the resentment they felt for police would find its way into their judgment. He smoothed down the lapels of his expensive suit and emanated an expression of finality.

"No more questions," he stated flatly and headed back to his chair. He and Brodie exchanged glances from across the room, a curious mixture of contempt and respect.

25

NEWSPAPERS, BOTH IN Phoenix and elsewhere, covered the trial on a daily basis. Every night on the television and radio were updates on any developments. The most startling statement of late was that of the lead defense. "Francis Mackey has decided to take the stand and provide his side of the events in a frank manner." This of course meant the professor would not be fully protected by the fifth amendment and was making his account subject to direct attack—a risky move for sure—but the die had been cast. Bantley went on not just to claim the innocence of his client, but extolling his qualities, referring to him as "the backbone of the State University history department."

Like a few million others, Ed Cudahy watched and listened to Bantley's announcement with some shock. He knew what he would do—with his nearly perfect attendance record at the high school, he could get away with missing a day or two and called into the office, claiming a medical appointment. Watching his former professor trying to get out of this jam was something he could not miss. Bantley's last words echoed in his head and Ed thought to himself, *If Mackey is the backbone, then the history department has scoliosis.*

He boarded an evening bus to Phoenix and stayed with his college friend Dan for the night. The two of them talked about old times and, of course, the Mackey case. Sure, Dan could drop him off downtown on his way to work, and do get back about what you saw and heard. The next morning, he treated Dan to breakfast, and then they drove near the courthouse, where Ed got off and proceeded through a security gate, glad he had left his pocketknife and pepper spray at home.

Walking down the hallways, he heard a female voice call out, "Mr. Cudahy!" Anyone calling him "mister" was either a student or former student, so he looked over his shoulder and saw the petite and pert young woman he remembered well.

"Darcie! So nice to see you."

He was reserved by nature, but she plunged into his arms with a warm hug, and he put his arms around her gently.

"I work upstairs in small claims. I tell everyone about you—the best teacher I ever had. I was talking to some old classmates a few weeks back, and we all talked about you. How every history class we took was a breeze—we knew the material already from your class. How have you been?"

"Not bad. Came down to catch some of the Mackey case. Have you seen any of it?" Ed asked, a bit embarrassed by her praise, but loving it nonetheless.

"You know, I did. Guy named Bryce, about your age, who knew the victim, said blackmail was in the works," Darcie replied, still smiling at the sight of her former teacher.

"Bryce? Can you describe him?"

Darcie paused, then said, "Really cute, glasses, and spoke with a very soft voice. The defense tore him to shreds."

"Was his last name Whorley, by any chance?" Ed asked with hesitation.

"Mm . . . sounds right . . . yes, I think the judge and defense called him that," Darcie answered slowly.

Hearing this, Ed pondered the memory of his childhood friend, spoke some more with Darcie, and they exchanged a big hug before parting.

Ed approached the courtroom with some caution. Not only was the accused someone he knew, albeit an enemy, so was one of the other figures involved in the case. He could not imagine his sixth-grade pal mixed up with anyone as sinister as Francis Mackey, but to think that his gentle friend crossed paths with a victim of a gruesome crime made him shudder. He entered the crowded room, found a seat, and waited for the show. Looking around, he thought he saw Francis Mackey, as he had looked ten years before in a priest's cleric. Ed realized this must be the younger brother mentioned in news articles.

After a few tense minutes, the bailiff's voice rang out with the routine announcement of the judge's arrival and all stood, waited a few seconds, and then resumed their seats. Virtually everyone then looked at the defendant, seated next to his attorney, looking small and scared next to the bigger man. Ed gazed at his former nemesis, noting that, for the first time he ever saw, Mackey was dressed properly, in a conservative suit, white shirt, and dark tie, though they both clashed slightly with the coat. At first, he thought Mackey was wearing a hat, and then realized it was a toupee that did not fit him correctly.

"Mr. Bantley, call your witness," Judge Sandlin's mellow voice rang out.

"The defense calls Francis DeSales Mackey."

The now ex-professor, recently resigned, approached the bench smoothly, was sworn in, and took his seat, fidgeting and trying to get comfortable. Bantley attempted to relax his client by speaking to him in a mild expression and nonthreatening gestures. He had Mackey tell the jury general information about himself, and then had him recreate the events of the fateful moment. Mackey told the same story he had told the police, of how he and Travis, along with Troy Anson, were together in Mackey's apartment one evening, and the atmosphere became angrier and hotter, both literally and figuratively, as Anson became irate at Travis about money owed by Travis to Anson.

"I knew Travis casually, had met him a few weeks previously. He also knew Troy, one of those decadent gays, hot-tempered and violent. Troy was not a friend, just an acquaintance. He had quite a cloudy past, a criminal I heard, and I am so sorry to have been associated with him. As the two of them started exchanging threats, I decided to get some ice cream to cool things off, no pun intended, and, while in the kitchen, I heard Travis yell. I ran out to the living room, and I saw that Anson had a gun in my hand—I mean, a gun in *his* hand," he quickly corrected himself.

A few eyebrows went up here and there at that slip, and Grant Bantley pursed his lips tightly and tried not to show anger. He longed for his bottle of whiskey. With an even-tempered voice, he said, "Continue, Mr. Mackey."

"The gun went off, not sure if Anson meant to fire, but Travis staggered, and Anson got closer and fired one more shot into the back of his head. I was stunned, sure he would shoot me next, so I decided to obey anything he said to spare my life. I rented the chainsaw and van later. Troy cut up the body while I cowed in a separate room, and then we carried the torso to Anson's car. He wrapped up the limbs in linen and told me to take them out and dump them somewhere secluded. Yes, I left the poor boy's extremities in some ivy, shaking in fear all the time. Anson said he was headed out to Mexico and said if the truth got out, he would kill me and my little brother. I deeply regret my failure to resist, or at least depart and report the shooting to the police, but my emotional status overruled all my logic."

There were a few follow-up questions, all benign, and the dynamic lawyer, drawing up his dignity, used all his resolve not to roll his eyes at what he had just heard, nodded, and moved away from the witness stand. With deference, he motioned for the cross-examination to begin.

Joel Penn, compared to Bantley, was much physically smaller and gave off the air of a scholar, appearing more like a professor than Francis Mackey did. Seemingly, no one would feel at all intimidated by the bespectacled man, with his neatly trimmed beard, but Mackey showed some fear, like a child confronted by a parent or teacher, who knows he has done wrong and been caught.

"Dr. Mackey, you say Troy Anson had been to your apartment before, and he knew Travis Kingman?"

"Yes, he knew Travis better than he knew me."

"But none of your neighbors had seen him, and none of Travis's friends and associates knew of him or anyone fitting the description you gave?" Penn continued.

"None of those that were questioned, perhaps. A more thorough investigation would have found someone who knew Anson."

"An entire team of homicide detectives worked for weeks on this case, as you may know," Penn stressed, speaking more to the jury than to the witness. Mackey did not respond.

"According to your testimony," the ADA continued, "Troy shot and killed Kingman, but not you. He sent you on some errands to gather the chainsaw, van, and such. Presumably, Anson stayed in your apartment while you fetched these. Did it ever occur to you just to cut and run, then call the police? Anson would have had no idea how to find you."

"That's what I should have done, but I panicked. He also threatened my brother." Mackey fiddled with his fingers as he answered.

"Your brother, who lives on the other side of the country, in a rectory, who has never been to Arizona before this?"

Mackey did not answer.

Joel Penn changed the line of questioning. "Professor, do you have any notion why Travis Kingman had, in his room, about two dozen photos, all taken in your apartment, showing him nude and one with the two of you together?"

Mackey halted a bit, then offered, "I took them, because he said he needed them to get into movies. The one of us together he said was because he wanted to show his family back in Kentucky that he had friends. There's no law against that," Mackey pushed back.

"No, nor should there be. Did you know that Travis Kingman was a minor?" Penn asked this question without the hint of accusation.

Sounding truthful for once, Mackey replied, "No, I did not know he was seventeen. He told me he was twenty, and he looked about like that, maybe even older. Also, all I did was take pictures of him . . . that's probably just a misdemeanor."

"So you assisted in carrying the torso to Anson's car, and disposing of at least the limbs, making you an accessory, which is a crime. Instead of dropping off the parts at the on-ramp, you could have driven away, called authorities, but instead you returned to your apartment and helped clean up the crime scene. Is that what you are saying you did?"

Mackey ground his teeth together and spoke with his familiar lisp, "Yes, I admit I was wrong, but I did not kill that boy."

"Mr. Mackey, did you tell a different story to the police before evidence showed that the blood in the chainsaw was human?" Penn asked this question to make Mackey's testimony even less tenable.

Hanging his head, Mackey tried to sound innocent.

"Yes, another regret of mine. I was so scared of Anson, or being blamed falsely for the crime, which has now happened, that I fabricated a tale of how we, Anson and I, ran over a pit bull belonging to a biker gang. I have since recanted that, and I lied out of fear."

From where he sat, a few yards away, Ed Cudahy could hear the drama in that old weasel voice, the pleading sound of someone who, heavy with guilt, was trying to convey the idea that he was the victim, not some poor seventeen-year-old runaway. Ed pinched the bridge of his nose, breathed deeply, and wished the old professor would just admit his wrongdoing and get the ordeal over with.

There were a few questions that followed, but Mackey's account had been thoroughly torpedoed by this time. Even Grant Bantley had to admit, silently, that his client had come across not just as guilty, but unbelievably stupid. He knew there had to be a game changer, and he had one waiting. When Judge Sandlin asked if the defense had any more business before adjourning for the day, Bantley stood up and addressed the court.

"Your honor, the defense has one more witness. Following the rules of discovery and disclosure, I will inform the prosecution at once, and I will call her at a time you appoint."

With a haggard look on his face, the judge announced a recess until the next afternoon, and tapped his gavel accordingly.

26

THE STATE RECEIVED from the defense all the needed information on who was to be, presumably, the last witness—Tabby Jeffer, known crystal meth addict and small-time criminal, the same ilk as Travis Kingman and millions of others. When she appeared in court, she wore long sleeves, many guessed to hide tattoos or needle marks, and tried to carry herself with some dignity. Her front teeth showed the damage of tweaking, and her gaze was distant with the lack of focus of someone who, no matter how much time has elapsed, still felt stoned. Penn knew what her testimony was all about—a last-ditch effort to make the jurors at least wonder if, maybe, the image of Troy Anson could be more than a specter, the actual perpetrator of the murder.

She was sworn in and took her seat. Everyone in the courtroom saw what had once been a pretty girl, with large expressive eyes, but ravaged by drugs and hard street life. Her tone of voice, as she answered Bantley's general questions, was monotone and clearly rehearsed. Yes, she knew Anson, had seen him in the company of that big guy with the Mohawk, and Anson was a mean and violent type. No, she did not know Francis Mackey, but knew that Travis had many customers, mostly older guys that he sponged off of. She had not seen Anson anytime lately, and had no idea where he may have disappeared to. Bantley thanked her politely and said to the prosecutor, "Your witness."

Joel Penn walked up within a few feet of the witness and spoke in a smooth and gentle voice. "Miss Jeffer, you say you knew an individual whose name, the best you knew, was Troy Anson?"

"Yes," she replied, her face vacuous and voice dull.

"Can you describe Mr. Anson for the jury? What did he look like?" Penn kept a manner of speaking that was just matter of fact.

"Well, he was young, twenties, about average height . . . your height, maybe." Tammy spoke these words with broken cadence, seeming to be searching for the answers.

"What color hair did he have?"

She hesitated a moment, then answered, "Um, blond hair . . . or light hair, anyhow."

"And you say you saw him with Travis Kingman?"

"Yeah, they were talking together a couple of times," she responded, with no emotion.

"Did Anson ever talk about Travis?"

"Yeah, said he owed him money."

"You mean Travis owed money to Anson, or . . . "

"Yeah, Travis had borrowed money from Troy."

"Miss Jeffer, do you have a history of drug abuse?"

"Objection!" Bantley bellowed out.

"Overruled," the judge spoke for the first time in several minutes.

"All right, I've been into crystal meth, and other drugs," she admitted, knowing that everyone in the courtroom figured that already.

Penn began his wrap up, asking, "Can you think of anyone else you might know, who saw Travis Kingman either with Mr. Anson, or you, or the accused?"

"Who?"

"The defendant, Dr. Mackey, seated here," and Penn motioned to the chair where Mackey sat.

After some drifting moments, she softly said, "No, guess not."

"That will be all," and the ADA walked back to his seat.

Judge Sandlin addressed the jury briefly about the recent testimony and then released them for a lunch break. The summation, he explained, would be presented later in the afternoon, marking the conclusion of the arguments, and then the jury would have to reach a verdict.

When everyone had settled back into the courtroom, Judge Sandlin ordered each side to sum up its closing arguments. Joel Penn, when his turn came, walked up to the jury, inhaled deeply, and began his case. He opened with a review of all the evidence, the statements made by Mackey and the defendant, and reminded them that only one man—Francis Mackey—was on trial here, not the police, and certainly not the victim.

"Dr. Mackey wants us to believe," he said, with a hint of disbelief, "that the murder occurred in his apartment, right in front of him, but that he was an innocent bystander. That this imaginary character found the professor's gun, which Mackey had bought only days before the killing and hid at least the cleaning kit in his office, and used it to kill Travis Kingman. Supposedly, Dr. Mackey was in fear for his own life, so he complies with the orders of someone he named Troy Anson. Anson lets an eyewitness run out the door, and Mackey goes to a convenience market, a van rental agency, and a hardware store over at least a six-hour period. Why didn't Mackey just run away, as far as he could, call the police? If he feared for his life, he could have jumped on a plane, headed out of state. Instead, he returns to the apartment, helps clean up, and then delivers the limbs, by himself, to a dump site.

"'He threatened my younger brother,' so he says. Assuming Anson did exist, how did he even know Dr. Mackey had a brother, let alone his name and where he lived? He was going to fly out to the East Coast, find the rectory, sneak in, and exact revenge? That is completely ridiculous.

"Here's another question," Penn spoke with almost a smile. "Dr. Mackey says that he left Anson alone in the apartment for a few hours, that Anson later cut up the body with the chainsaw, and that Anson disposed of the torso. Why would Anson do that? Wouldn't he just take off, leave the bloody mess in Mackey's apartment, let Mackey try to cover up the tracks while Anson disappeared? No one could have connected Anson to the crime."

Bantley's eyes floated over to the jury box and tried to read their thinking. Some expressions seemed to say, silently, "Yeah, of course."

"As if that is not completely absurd," Penn continued, "Mackey spends days trying to act normal, and when questioned by the police, fabricates a story about the blood on the chainsaw being that of a dog. He later drops that account in favor of a different one, admits to being at least an accessory to a murder, and hopes someone will believe him.

"Consider all of the blood evidence and the testimony of Mr. Quincy, the hardware store clerk, and Mr. McKeevy, the truck driver, all of it completely *uncontested* by the defense." Penn stressed the word *uncontested* with gusto, almost a smirk, to convey that neither Mackey or Bantley had denied any of it.

Penn knew that he was not legally bound to establish motive, but without it, the jury might totter. He decided not to push the extortion angle, since he knew Bantley would point out that Bryce Whorley's testimony was inconclusive, so he took a path of a much more general nature.

"Members of the jury, this"—pointing to Mackey—"is a man who acted in rage, pure rage, and knowingly took the life of a seventeen-year-old. He bought a gun to kill Travis and rented a chainsaw, by himself, to dismember the remains. That he destroyed evidence, scoured off blood, disposed of remains, and lied about his actions all show proves his guilt," he stated matter-of-factly.

After discussing the case in broad terms, the ADA spoke of the victim.

"This is not just the case of one runaway. This was the murder of an innocent minor, taken by surprise, set up, defenseless, lured into Dr. Mackey's trap, and his body desecrated. For this young man's family, and for all of us, you must deliver a verdict of guilty. Thank you."

Nick Brodie had gotten lucky that day. He had answered a call to locate a lost child, headed out of the office, and it was soon revealed that the little girl had curled up onto a pile of linens in the laundry room and fallen asleep, unknown to her distraught mother. This freed up most of his afternoon, so he hurried to the courtroom to catch the summations. He found himself nodding his head in agreement with every statement made by the prosecution, knowing this could be and should be an easy guilty verdict. When he saw Grant Bantley stand before the judge and jury with that pompous expression of his, he thought of the old joke: "What's the difference between a dead possum in the middle of the road and a dead lawyer in the middle of the road? The skid marks before the possum."

Grant Bantley, big and imposing, paused before beginning his oration, looking confident and aggressive. When he spoke, his rich bass voice carried across the room and rang with resonance. "This was, indeed, a gruesome crime. A seventeen-year old juvenile delinquent and an unrepentant racist ends up shot to death and dismembered. So what do the police do? They grab a convenient scapegoat. Not because he did it, but because they think they can get a guilty verdict and catch a big fish, make themselves look good. That is all this case is about. They have hung a noose around Professor Mackey, dragged him in here to offer him up as a sacrifice, while the real killer roams free.

"There is not one eyewitness. No one saw what happened that tragic evening. Yes, plenty of blood, but nothing to indicate that the defendant shot Travis Kingman. In fact, Professor Mackey may have been the next victim had he not obeyed the commands of the murderer. If you are thinking he should have done this or that instead, consider the emotional state he must have been in, one of shock." Bantley paused, shifted, and began his next appeal.

"You are expected to believe that this highly educated man, sixty years old, with no criminal record, not even a misdemeanor, suddenly springs up and commits murder. This gentleman, known by his colleagues as 'St. Francis' and 'Mack the Mollifier' for his disdain of conflict and confrontations, who backs down from any challenge, instantly becomes a one-man killing machine. Five years before a comfortable retirement, and he throws it all away like this? Had he been a career criminal, with the toughness to match, you might believe the accusations, but think of how unlikely it is that he could have committed this act," Bantley offered, his tone softening somewhat.

Bantley pressed on. "Mr. Mackey is not a big or a strong man. He is not the handy type who knows to fix things around the house, use tools, and other such skills. He is, by his own admission, a bumbler, who could not have operated the chainsaw, an observation made by Rhett Quincy, who testified earlier about the day the chainsaw was rented."

He continued, "As I said, he is well educated, holding a doctoral degree, with published works and hailed as a scholar nationwide. Very intelligent and cognizant of the legal process, being a historian. So why would someone of his intellect buy a gun with the intent to murder someone from a legal gun store, sign the paper work, and leave a trail? Wouldn't a criminal plotting a crime buy the gun from a private source or under a false name? Yes, he rented the chainsaw, but Anson returned it, with the professor assuming the blood had been removed from the inner chambers. That is a plausible account."

Bantley made eye contact with the two Latino jurors and played his last ace. "Like always, the police target a member of a group they hold in low esteem. In the same fashion that they discriminate against racial minorities, they persecute Francis Mackey because of his sexual orientation and stall in their efforts to find the true culprit. Here is your chance to show them how wrong they are," Bantley said, breathing audibly.

The rest of the summation was a lecture on reasonable doubt, sprinkled with several effective analogies, hoping that at least one juror would pause just enough to hold out on a guilty verdict. He summarized with a canned conclusion, one he had used many times over the years, and bowed his head. The courtroom remained silent for a few seconds.

Judge Sandlin's calm voice broke the quiet. "Members of the jury, you have heard both sides. Tomorrow morning you will deliberate as a group. Do not discuss the case with anyone, not even your family." He followed with the same general instructions as he always did, tapped his gavel, and the courtroom cleared.

27

TABBY JEFFER SAT in the doughnut shop and stared out the window into the street, looking blankly at parked cars. Following instructions, she looked only forward, while munching on sugary twists and sipping her hot cocoa. She added some sugar to the drink, hoping the sweetness would calm her cravings. From her peripheral vision, she saw the two bikers enter the store, walk to the counter, and order bear claws. On the backs of their vests was a red devil's head, with flames encircling it. One took the bear claws out of the white paper bag as they slowly moved near her table, while the second inserted two envelopes into the recently emptied bag. Without looking at her, nor she at them, the bag was placed softly to her side. The bigger one spoke in a low snarl that was barely audible but still threatening, "You never saw us. Word ever gets out, we stomp you into the shit."

There was no nodding or any acknowledgment. Tabby kept her focus on the street while the two bikers exited, mounted their hogs, kick-started and melded into the traffic flow. Tabby waited for them to leave, then eagerly grabbed the bag, reached for the envelope she hoped held the meth, and dreamed of what she would do with the money from the other.

Within walking distance at that moment, the courtroom stirred to life. Judge Sandlin calmed everyone down and again instructed the jury about their duty to reach a verdict. They were to choose a foreman, discuss the evidence, and vote by ballot. If not unanimous, talk and vote again later. Any snags, continue working, but do not give in against your conscience.

The twelve jurors walked upstairs to a separate chamber. The foreman, a husky Hispanic self-employed businessman, led the group and asked for any input. Most at the table were quiet, but questions arose about the possibility or probability of Mackey's explanations, off and on. Some wondered about motive, and all discussed the chainsaw, the sightings of Mackey, and his attempts to place the blame on another party. After about an hour, a ballot was taken.

The foreman slowly counted off the ballots for everyone in the room to see—eleven to one. The one holdout, a retired high school teacher, spoke in a reserved voice about some of his doubts. Talk continued about the hidden cleaning kit, the testimony of Gavin McKeevy and Rhett Quincy, all stating that the accused was alone in his efforts to hide evidence and cover up his guilt. The foreman then read aloud some of the transcripts of the testimony of Mackey and others, and by the end of the readings, the former teacher spoke out, "Okay, I'll change my vote."

The foreman notified the bailiff, and the twelve were herded down the hall and to the elevators. No one spoke at this point; their demeanor was beyond calm, almost chilling.

As the jurors filed into the courtroom, a soft buzzing of voices arose, and Judge Sandlin rapped his gavel for quiet. All eyes were on the twelve, and there seemed no indication of the verdict, based on their expressions. They assumed their seats, and the judge spoke to them briefly, words long since largely memorized, and asked the foreman and the defendant to rise. Grant Bantley stood stolidly by the professor, an odd couple, one small, bespectacled man next to his attorney, tall, strong and assertive.

"Members of the jury . . . "—all in the room simply tuned out the standard address, awaiting the voice of the foreman, which they soon heard, deep and steady, once the judge wrapped up with—"so say you one, so say you all?"

"We the jury, find the defendant, Francis DeSales Mackey"—the next second seemed like an hour—"guilty of the murder of Travis Neughton Kingman." Chatter pervaded throughout the room, making the rest of the words less audible. There were signs of relief, even glee, but not a hint of reaction from either of the lawyers. Mackey stared down at the floor, a look of shame on his face, that of someone who has just been told by his peers that they knew what he had done and had believed none of his story.

Joel Penn and his staff shook hands with one another, smiling and relieved. Father Damien Mackey dropped his head into his hands and looked almost like a mirror image of his brother. Reporters scribbled down particulars and left to announce the news while the judge continued to provide instructions for the jury.

Judge Sandlin asked Mackey and Bantley to stand once more for the sentencing. As expected, he announced that Dr. Mackey was sentenced to lifetime imprisonment, with eligibility for parole in ten years. Two deputies approached Mackey to escort him to his cell, but before they could apply the handcuffs, Mackey turned to his younger brother, waved, and tried to convey a gesture of gratitude. The professor and his escorts disappeared, and the courtroom was soon cleared.

28

ED CUDAHY RACED home from his last history class and down to his house, within walking distance of the high school. He turned on his TV set and planted himself on the sofa while it warmed up. Seconds later, the image of Mackey appeared, the bailiff's voice announcing the verdict, seeming far off. Ed saw the guilt on his old professor's face and actually felt some pity for him, even though he saw justice being served.

On the outskirts of Phoenix, Gavin McKeevy was waiting for his load, and he, too, watched the verdict delivered, sitting along with other truckers in the coffee room. How much impact had his testimony carried? Had he changed the outcome? Almost certainly, this was a once-in-a-lifetime occurrence, a story he would tell for years to come, his children, or grandchildren.

Bryce Whorley was too distracted to concentrate on the news of the trial. He had heard snippets of the verdict, almost regretted his testimony, and the emotional stress it had caused, but that, too, seemed small now. Summoning up his courage, he picked up the phone and called his parents in Mesa.

His mother answered, and after some small talk, he told her, "Mom, I'll be checking into the hospital tomorrow morning. They're going to run a series of tests on me, find out what's wrong. Keep you posted." He hung up, feeling a great weight on his shoulders, and looked downcast. He was not sure if he could keep his parents notified, or if he could tell the truth he so heavily dreaded.

Nick Brodie and his staff were celebrating at Duffy's, their favorite bar, watching replays on the mounted television set. The air was filled with victory, thinking what all cops think at such a point—one more scumbag taken off the streets and locked up, as he and all the others should be. Button and McIntosh instructed others to quiet down while they proposed a toast to the chief detective. Raising their glasses, they spoke in unison.

"For you, Brodie!"

Nick looked downward as he lifted his own glass, seeming modest even, and thought to himself, silently, *And for you, Travis.*

Grant Bantley had a toasting of his own, so to speak. All alone, in his dark office, he broke out the Irish whiskey he had intended to use to celebrate the acquittal of a man he knew was guilty. Downing glass after glass, he felt soporific, knowing that a zombie-like fog would take over as the evening progressed, and dreamed of his next chance to grab the limelight.

"One more round," he spoke to the dim room.

29

L IKE MANY OTHER Phoenix residents, Ed Cudahy followed along in the newspapers about the aftermath of the case in the months that followed the verdict. There had been other homicide cases he had studied closely, but none had touched him more personally. He read about Grant Bantley's claims of miscarriage of justice and his vow to appeal the case, along with quotes from Father Damien Mackey extolling his brother's virtues, when an article on the opposite page caught his eye.

The article spoke of a "new" disease, and how it had claimed the lives of some locals. Prominently featured was an account of Phoenix dancer and actor, Bryce Whorley, originally from Mesa, age thirty-two. His death had been accelerated somehow, perhaps from an unrelated operation, and AIDS had ended his life in much quicker time than most other patients. The article also mentioned how Whorley had been a nonmaterial witness in the Mackey case, recently ended. It included a quote from his father: "We knew of his sexual orientation, and never approved of it, but he was our son and we loved him dearly, always will."

Those words largely echoed what Ed was thinking. An ardent Catholic and social conservative, he sometimes felt resentment towards homosexuals, but reminded himself to be compassionate. He found that easier for him to do regarding his sixth-grade friend than the college professor who had so antagonized him.

He reminisced back to when he and Bryce were both twelve. They had a dream of donning red sports coats and taking the stage at the talent show as their favorite TV comic duo, but it never came to pass. One of many regrets, Ed thought. But he would never regret Bryce being his friend in those lonely days.

Ed also reflected on his relationship with the surly professor, so long ago it seemed, but only ten years back. In spite of the insults and irritating mannerisms, he wondered if there was not some good, some decency, like what Mackey's younger brother had mentioned. Should he harbor those ill feelings, or try to make peace with the past?

He read the remainder of the Mackey article, stating how Francis Mackey would be, presumably, transferred to a prison outside of town called Mare Creek, with high-level security. The best solution Ed could come up with, the question of whether or not he should communicate with his former professor, now a convict, was to sit on this for a while, and allow some time for thought.

30

One year after the murder.

A NOTHER SCHOOL YEAR had ended for Ed Cudahy. Like many teachers, once they had more than ten years in the classroom racked up, he knew that he would spend his entire career teaching, and hopefully at the same school. Then, before he was too old to enjoy it, face a comfortable retirement.

He often referred to his summer time off as a "practice retirement," thinking of the old joke, "What are the three best things about teaching? June, July, and August!" This year, he had planned and was just getting started on his getaway, a long trek across the country in his pickup with a camper shelf to the East Coast and back, seeing historical sights and national parks. It was while dreaming of the escapade that an announcement on the radio captured his attention—"Francis Mackey, convicted killer, denied appeal." He listened to the rest and then worked up his courage for the task he would tackle before taking his excursion.

He looked up the mailing address for Mare Creek State Prison, jotted it down, and sat at the desk where he did all his paperwork. After careful contemplation, he penned the words from his heart, an effort to connect with Francis Mackey, a man he knew was a murderer, but whom Ed still wanted to reach out to and make some gesture of peace. He began plainly, with "Dear Dr. Mackey, I hope you remember me . . . "

It was not easy for him, but the words gradually flowed, slowly, and he folded up the stationery paper, inserted it into an envelope, and biked over to the neighborhood post office. After dropping it off, Ed stared at the mailbox for a few seconds, still unsure if his decision was prudent or not, and then turned away and headed home.

The days that followed seemed like a long time, and Ed thought of little else but the words he had written down, and the anticipated reply from Mare Creek's most notorious inmate. He felt some fear of . . . rejection? A mean-spirited response from Mackey? Ed knew from experience how harsh the man could be. Hard words were nothing new to him, but someone as sensitive as Ed always feared criticism and rebuffs.

After about a week, the prison response came. With some trepidation, Ed opened the envelope, found a simple slip of paper and, on it, scrawled just one word—"Sure." Just "sure," not some words of surprise or a rebuke, anything to clarify what Mackey was thinking? The initials "F.M." appeared at the bottom. Not much to go on, but Ed then took the next steps.

He wrote a formally worded letter to the officials at the prison, stating his intent. He was not sure if getting clearance to visit a convicted murderer was more difficult than trying to visit a prisoner of a lesser offense, but he was patient and waited for an answer, which came in about five days. It was bureaucratic in style, not surprisingly, and provided instructions, the hours allowed for visitation, rules restricting contact, and directions to the facility. Ed made careful note of all the information, and said a few prayers to calm himself and to prepare for this confrontation . . . no, that was not the right word, this encounter, where he sought to find some answers for himself and perhaps Mackey as well.

Ed started up his truck in the driveway and headed out to Jackson Road. He knew the way to the prison well, because it was on the road that led to Lake Apache, one of his favorite fishing spots. He passed a gated bedroom community, veered to the right past some horse enclosures, and turned again at the railroad crossing. The facilities were about halfway between Phoenix and his home in the northern part of the state. He parked in the visitors lot and approached the forbidding looking entry. It was an austere building, with the trademark razor wire atop a high fence, and towers with sentries posted. Ed walked toward the visitor center.

There was, of course, paperwork to be filled out, and instructions about the parameters of the visit. The guards all looked bored and spoke in perfunctory tones, barely looking at Ed, even though the inmate he planned to visit must be a celebrity of some degree, or at least the type that anyone who worked there would be wary of. He passed through security gates similar to those found at an airport, emptied out his pockets, and one of the guards waved something over his body like a paddle, then gently patted around his pockets. Satisfied, they pointed Ed the way to a stark waiting area. After twenty minutes, he heard his name called on the intercom and was ushered into a row of seats with wall-mounted telephones and a hard, clear plastic—not glass—partition separating the visitors from the inmates.

Ed squirmed a bit in the uncomfortable chair, anxious for the meeting and uncertain about how it would develop. When the door behind the partition opened and Francis Mackey entered, now seeming older and fatigued, escorted by a taciturn guard, his waiting ended, and he rose partly to greet his former teacher, started to offer to shake hands until he remembered the glass between them. For once, Mackey wore clothes that matched—all orange. It was the first time Ed had seen his teacher's head uncovered, partly bald, but splotched unevenly with gray hairs, like a poorly mowed lawn. The two nodded to each other and reached for the phones at the same time. Ed was always a bit slow at greetings, so it was Mackey who spoke first.

"Well, hello," Mackey began in his soft but irritating voice. "The paper they handed me said 'Eamon,' so I was unsure for a spell, then realized it must be you. How has life been treating you?"

"Oh, pretty good, overall. As you may know, I became a high school history teacher. Before that, I worked for a department store, hated it, then at the IRS processing center, just for the tax season.

Tried the phone company briefly, then went back to State to get a secondary teaching credential."

And Ed paused a bit, when Mackey interrupted him, not too sharply. "Oh, yes, I remember bumping into you at some buffet for the social studies department, and you told me you were working on a credential, student teaching and such," his old professor commented, sounding like a whiner.

Ed felt a flashback to that exact moment, recalling the buffet. When Mackey said, "bumping into you," that could be taken literally, because he remembered standing at the table, and feeling an elbow roughly jamming into his upper arm, pretending to be inadvertent when, in fact, it was completely intentional—Mackey's peculiar way of getting attention. Ed had been surprised his onetime teacher had remembered him from four years before. He could still see the sloppily dressed man, freeloading off the buffet table, cramming crackers and cheese into his mouth, while the crumbs fell, lodging in Mackey's week-old whiskers, with some falling onto his mismatched sweater. Ed had politely engaged him in small talk before making himself scarce.

His focus returned to the present, and he addressed a man who seemed so old, although only in his early sixties.

"Well, it's been great. I teach at an all-girls Catholic high school. Almost all of the students go to college, They're very highly motivated, and discipline problems are almost nonexistent. Every Sunday, I can't wait to get back to the classroom. Most of my coworkers are very nice, and it's highly autonomous. There couldn't be a better job for me anywhere," Ed spoke, his voice lifting and taking some animation.

Mackey seemed impressed, then responded with some compunction. "It sounds idyllic, although I doubt it offers much in the way of remunerative value."

"No, I could make more in public schools, and better benefits, but I wouldn't last long there. Classroom control is my weakness, and the kids in those schools, most of them, don't behave so well," Ed added.

He continued, "Oh, you know how the class I took from you was about historical research? You might like to know that I put some of those skills to use, since my high school is really big into research papers, with footnotes, primary sources, and bibliographies. Not just content."

Mackey nodded, his face displaying some appreciation.

Ed drew up his courage, as he looked down a bit and tried a soft and encouraging tone of voice. This was the main reason he had come to this prison—something that, if he had not done, or at least tried to do, it would haunt him forever. "You know, Mr. Mackey, we were both brought up in the same faith. I'm sure there are Catholic chaplains here you could speak to, to help you make peace with everything." These words drifted from him with strain.

Mackey spoke up, "If you mean confession, in the religion sense, I don't believe in that anymore, and have nothing to confess to anyway. You heard me deny wrongdoing at the trial."

"I'm not judging you, just hoping you can make peace. You admitted at the trial to have made some mistakes, so you could get any guilt off your conscience if you make the effort. I know I have, with my many regrets," Ed followed.

Mackey shook his head with disdain, and muttered, "You and my brother, one and the same. He lives in his rectory, thinks he knows what the real world is like. At least he is one who has never deserted me."

Ed picked up on this. "Your brother, then. You could speak to him in absolute privacy and confidence, clear things up . . . "

The professor butted in rudely, as he had often done, held up one hand as if to ward his former student off. "Ed, we're done, we're done," Mackey barked in anger. "This is over with, no more." He motioned for the uniformed guard to escort him back to his cell.

As Mackey arose, he took one, last fleeting glance at Ed Cudahy, and spoke in his nasal twang, "And I must say, you are still the only person I have known to have whistled in class."

Cudahy sat still for a few moments before gathering himself up and heading out to the parking lot. He climbed into his pickup truck, stared at the dirty floor mats, and thought heavily for a few minutes before turning the key. Another page in his life, left partly unwritten. He drove home through the winding roads, the image of Francis Mackey in his orange jumpsuit lodged in his memory.

31

Ten years after the murder.

THE THICK, SOFTBOUND notebook featured the title of the class prominently on the cover—"Exploring the Internet: An Introduction." Ed Cudahy held it in his hands, the information and steps still new to him. Only about two years ago, he wondered, both silently and sometimes out loud, "What the hell *is* the internet?" He had read newspaper and magazine articles about cyberspace and domains, whatever they were, and knew, if he wanted to survive another twenty years of teaching, he better get with the program.

His first encounter with the internet came while taking a different class from the same private college, one on the history of Lake Havasu. He had stopped by to visit his sister's family, and one of the nephews had obtained some information for him on his home computer. He let the nephew do all the work, asked him to print out the data for him, and still remained baffled by what he had just witnessed. But at least it was a step. Now the father of a five-year-old boy, Teddy, he also knew that he would have to help enable his son to become computer functional to be successful in the future.

His new skill, though tenuous, had already played a vital role in his life. While following along in the guide, the type where the student learns at home, he had researched on his PC about Uncle Eamon, his mother's older brother, the man for whom he had been named. No one had heard anything from Eamon Shelley in years, and many wondered what had become of him. Not hearing from him was no shock, since he had distanced himself from his family, especially after Ed's mother had passed on, but when Ed's dad called Eamon's phone number and strangers answered, a dark feeling came over everyone. Searching through social security records, he discovered that the lost uncle had died five years previously, and no one had ever been notified. The first thing Ed did was to call up his Uncle Charlie, his mom's younger brother, with the news, which saddened Charlie, even though he had been at odds with Eamon for years, and had largely written him off.

He had heard how you could also read up on current affairs by using search engines, another term Ed had to ask about. With much hesitation, he would ask, "You mean, I could type in, say, 'bass fishing in Montana,' and there it would be?" His younger and more tech savvy coworkers just nodded and smiled. With this new ability in mind, and just a touch of skepticism, Ed Cudahy decided to find out what had become of Professor Francis Mackey, no longer a front-page item, just someone still spoken of in tones of disgust and astonishment. Following the text sent him, he entered Mackey's full name (in quotation marks, he had heard would narrow the search down) and see if any information arose. In a few seconds, a list of articles appeared, with details about the last stages of Mackey's life.

"Convicted Chainsaw Murderer, 70, Dies In Prison," read one, while another stated "College Professor, Killer, Dead From AIDS." He read the articles thoroughly, not skipping a word, and chewing over his memories of the trial and of the times he had crossed with Mackey, when Cudahy was only in his twenties. All discussed the case, the killing of a seventeen-year-old runaway, the dismemberment, discovery of the remains, and the subsequent trial. Not many new details were revealed to Ed, but one article included a quote from a childhood friend of Francis Mackey, citing their hometown in Minnesota. This opened a new door of curiosity, and Ed Cudahy, like the history buff he was, continued to search for information about the town, Duluth, which he knew nothing about and had never even been near. He made it to some sites about graduating high school classes throughout the decades and located portions of Mackey's senior yearbook.

Finally, he came to the portraits of each student posed for his graduation photo, and each with a caption including name and high school activities. He could barely recognize seventeen-year-old Francis Mackey, with a full head of hair, swept back and gathered up in a curl, similar to what Ed's father had sported back in the forties. Other than the trial, it was the only time he had ever seen Mackey neatly dressed, in a herringbone suit and a bow tie was the bow tie a reflection of Harry Truman, the new president back at that time? What was perplexing, most of all, was the fact that the young Francis Mackey, unlike most graduating students, was not smiling, but looked, in fact, quite pensive. What was on the mind of this young man, who would later turn into a cynical professor and killer? His full name, "Francis DeSales Mackey," appeared below, and an address somewhere in East Duluth, which meant nothing to Ed, since he did not know the town at all, but tried to picture his home, where he lived with his younger brother. Also listed were the groups to which he had belonged—Drama Club, Coin Club, Camera Club, and such, and Ed wondered if his old teacher had really been involved with other students, or Mackey may have just signed up so he would have something impressive for the yearbook, building a resume early in life. Another irony that hit him was to think, here was Francis Mackey, at seventeen, the same age Travis was when he fell to Mackey's bullets.

Ed thumbed through his textbook some more, trying to learn more searching techniques, following instructions carefully. For his next practice, he looked up information on names posted on the Vietnam Memorial in Washington, DC. He was not sure if he knew anyone personally who had died over there, but he searched for those killed in the early '70s, perhaps upperclassmen who had been drafted or enlisted. The war was winding down by the time Ed started high school, and the treaty to end American involvement signed only about a month after he turned eighteen. Finding no familiar names or anyone he knew from Mesa or Louisville, he sat back and breathed softly for a few moments.

Thinking of the war made Ed recall his cousin, Don Cudahy, who had served and made it back. Word had gotten around that Don had died from AIDS in his adopted home town of Cincinnati, so Ed started searching for information on Don, the most mixed-up person he had ever known in his life. Somehow, Don had gotten the idea that he (with linen-white skin and pale-blue eyes) was black. Don's brother, Fred, a Mormon who had mapped out the family genealogy, tried to explain to his younger brother that this could not be the case, but there was no convincing him, so Don grew out his hair Afro-style and claimed African heritage.

As if that were not enough uncertainty, Don also, for no apparent reason, also decided he was Jewish and began to study Hebrew and Talmud. How a Kentucky-born Baptist whose ancestors dated back before the days of Daniel Boone could be a Jew was yet another mystery, but cousin Don had made up his mind.

Then, Don, who had been a considerable ladies' man in his youth and married and then divorced twice, came to the conclusion, after a trip to San Francisco and romping in the Tenderloin, that he was no longer a heterosexual and should, as some would say, "come out of the closet." From that point on, Don carried a purse and added a swishing sashay to his gait. If anyone had ever desired to suffer among the persecuted, becoming a black, Jewish homosexual would definitely have done the trick.

Ed knew his cousin had died of AIDS, or as critics would say, "His lifestyle and decisions killed him," but sought the information about his final years, and found the obituary. It spoke of Donald Paul Cudahy, known as "Mr. Cheese" in his community because of his job stocking the shelves of grocery stores with vast assortments of cheeses, had succumbed to complications resulting from AIDS, and was survived by a brother in Kentucky and a daughter (Ed had never met her) in Virginia.

After a few days of respite, Ed decided to continue his research. There had been, as he had read and heard in the media, numerable efforts to honor the victims of AIDS, similar to monuments for honoring Americans killed in past wars. Instead of a wall, the proposed memorial would be in the form of a large quilt, made up of patches, each with the name of a victim, and some artistic display reflecting something about the person (most of them male) that had been noteworthy. Still a bit awkward, he found a database and began his work.

It felt mildly uncomfortable, typing in his own last name, but he quickly found the only Cudahy on the list, and located an image of the one square dedicated to his lost cousin. On a field of chartreuse he found, "Donald P. Cudahy." To the right of his name, a wedge of swiss cheese, with the caption, "Mr. Cheese" below it. It struck Ed odd that a man's life, even a short one, would convey only what he did in his last few years, ignoring a hitch in the navy and being a father and small-time businessman.

Since he had not gotten as close to Don as he had to most of his other cousins on his father's side, the thought of this life ended did not affect him as personally as his next goal, to find the section dedicated to his childhood friend, someone who had been a big and bright part of his life thirty years before, when he had felt so alone.

He did not know his friend's middle name, the subject had never come up, but with both an unusual first and last name, it did not take long for Ed to reach Bryce's square. "Bryce E. Whorley," it read, and he wondered if the "E" stood for "Edward" (the English equivalent of his own first name), and if there had been a loose common bond previously unknown. Below the name was a silhouette of a vaudeville dancer, replete with boater hat and cane, a genuine hoofer of old. How appropriate, Ed thought, thinking of Bryce's love of theater and dancing. Bryce's name and the outline of the dancer appeared on a background of pale lavender, vibrant and absorbing.

His memory drifted back to sixth grade, where he found camaraderie with only one other classmate, Bryce, the "sissy" in the class, who greeted Ed, "the fat kid," every morning before school and engaged him in talk about their favorite TV shows and shared many laughs. Had he known his friend would be dead in twenty years, by his early thirties, would he have treasured those times more? Or . . . ?

Ed sat in his recliner and watched his five-year-old son at his small play table with his toy police cars, making drawings of them, and talking about his day in kindergarten. Father and son, a strong but complicated bond, and Ed wondered if Bryce's father had been looking at his own son and having the same feelings decades earlier. Did that poor runaway, Travis, even have a father? He did not know. How about Mackey's dad? Did it ever occur to him that his son was a homosexual, let alone one who led a seedy secret life and would resort to butchery?

Ed drew a folding chair closer to his son's play space and watched Teddy tinker with his toys. A boy, a beautiful child, with a pink angel face. What would his only son become, as years passed, eventually into adulthood? Had the fathers of Dr. Mackey and Travis done anything wrong, or was there any way they could have molded their sons, guided them the right way? Could he being doing anything differently right now"

He could only wonder.

About the Author

E. WAYNE CUNDIFF (Ed) was born in Newport, Rhode Island and has lived in many states and provinces. He taught high school history with joy for thirty-five years and is now semi-retired. He loves travel, fishing, reading and has been a life-long trivia buff. He lives with his wife in California, and they have a son in Wisconsin.

CPSIA information can be obtained
at www.ICGtesting.com
Printed in the USA
LVHW04s1221030918
588991LV00003B/25/P